Ray Anthony was born in Kingston Jamaica in 1958 and lived with his grandparents until 1968, when he came to Britain to join his parents. Educated in south London, when he had the choice, he studied only maths and science - he found the arts crushingly boring. His first employment was in retail management, then he joined the Royal Air Force. After leaving the Royal Air Force he changed career to media sales management. It was during this time that he discovered he had a hidden creative bent. *'Less of my time was being spent on selling or managing, and more on shuffling pieces of paper. Writing strategic reports did my brain in, so I started 'jazzing them up'. The bosses were not amused. If I wanted to keep my job* and *my sanity, I had to find some release.'* In 1987 he started writing his first novel. He is now a media sales consultant and finds that training salespeople gives him ample scope to exercise his theatrical predisposition.

Also by Ray Anthony

Science Fiction
Interdictor - Book One of **The Unknowable Enemy** *Trilogy*
Armour - Book Two of **The Unknowable Enemy** *Trilogy*
Pilot
Empress

Contemporary Fiction
All Woman
Interface

Non Fiction Humour
Thinking Man's Guide To Pregnancy, Childbirth & Fatherhood

CAPTAIN

The Unknowable Enemy

BOOK THREE

Ray Anthony

ACE - London

ISBN 978 1 8382975 3 4

ACE
PO Box 10289
London SW17 9ZF

www.acebooksonline.com

Chapter 1

This was *her* ship! And when she took command of *her* ship, she wanted to walk onto *her* bridge with the crew being called to attention, 'Captain on deck!' However, fresh from the Janneri shipyards, the heavy cruiser *Kumasi* was also the designated flagship of the ground support flotilla of the reconstituted ninth fleet. As a matter of form, Commodore Axford had transferred his flag to *Kumasi* although *Kumasi* wasn't yet able to perform the role of a flagship. Because of that fact, the very first time she'd set foot on *her* ship, she'd been summoned to Axford, decked out in her number one dress uniform like some fresh-out-of-the-academy midshipman.

Pissed off! She was right royally pissed off and was trying to reign-in and bottle her annoyance before she appeared in front of her immediate superior. She'd come across Axford before although not serving directly under him. Even so, she knew he was one tough old son-of-a-bitch; you'd never put the fate of the boys and girls planetside in the hands of a cautious commander. By the time she'd neared Flotilla OpsCen she'd gained a modicum of composure as it gradually dawned on her that it probably wouldn't aid crew morale to see the band-new captain of their brand-new ship stomping past them like a demented zombie intent on ripping out someone's liver with their bare hands.

Of course, this wasn't her first command, or even her second for that matter, but she'd *earned* this ship. A heavy cruiser and not just any heavy cruiser but one destined to be at the sharp end - close support for planetary assaults - a big stick! Taking command of a ship like this had been her singular goal since the day she graduated, and that once-in-a-lifetime 'moment' had been officiously and discourteously snatched from her… The two marine guards at the entrance to the Flotilla OpsCen standing even more erect at her approach hinted that she hadn't calm down enough, and there was nothing she could do to assuage it.

Stepping into the OpsCen she'd expected to be greeted by the commodore and the usual command staff but also seated with him was the new boss of the ninth fleet, Admiral of the Fleet Rahumaehullah: he'd inherited the fleet from the recently decreased, Admiral of the Fleet Choi-Tan. Even more dauntingly, also present was the overall boss, Admiral of the Fleet Akobundu-Tan.

Captain Magambál Talberg instantly felt overawed.

"Please be seated, Captain." Before she could salute, Axford waved her into a seat that had rotated to face the three 'big beasts'. Two Admirals of the Fleet? She'd never been in a situation where she'd even witnessed two of them in the same space. As a matter of fact, she'd make an educated guess that there were standing orders which prohibited such an occurrence - to prevent all the 'strategic assets' being taken out in one sitting. As she sat, she noted the movement of the two Admirals' eyes; they were obviously reading text from a one-way hologram. Now rather self-conscious, she had a strong inkling as to whom the said text pertained.

"You're not in an intimate relationship and haven't been in any type of *association* beyond the professional or the distantly platonic for several years, Captain." In cutting to the chase, Axford signalled that this 'interview' was going to be short and sweet.

How, the Hell, did they know that?! They'd dragged her away from *her* bridge over this BS?

"With due respect…"

"A celibate captain wedded solely to their ship: unencumbered by anything meaningfully conjugal or affecting, steadfastly dedicated to duty..." Admiral Rahumaehullah arched an eyebrow, steepled his hands beneath his chin and paternally lent towards her. "...How terribly European."

Was this some kind of test? "Sir, I must protest..."

"Where are you from, Captain?" Smiling, again Rahumaehullah cut her off.

"Earth, S..."

"That much is obvious, where exactly on Earth?" This time it was Axford who interrupted.

Too much was happening too fast with some seriously senior officers; she sucked in a slow breath to buy thinking time. "I'm from Balatonszemes, it's in central Europe."

"And do we, the modern navy - the space navy - follow the European tradition, Captain?"

"No, Sir."

"If we do not follow European naval tradition, with which exemplar do we associate?"

Now she had a sense of where this might be leading, and she desperately needed to head it off. "The Polynesian paradigm, Sir: a hierarchical command structure with inter-connecting personal relationships based on a family/village grouping of about a hundred and forty individuals in total but with twenty, or thereabouts, of the relationships being intimate."

"Define for us, if you please, your understanding of the term 'an intimate relationship'." Commodore Axford radiated feigned patience.

She always had an intimate relationship with her First Officer, senior staff and anyone who regularly manned the bridge, but that wasn't what they were alluding to. Then again, you didn't get to be the captain of a capital ship by being a shrinking violet and just rolling over in front of your bosses because they were more senior to you. "There is a clear distinction between the intimate and the personal..."

"If you think I intend to have one of my capital ships being commanded by a sexually dysfunctional emotional cripple, think again Captain." Admiral Rahumaehullah hadn't raised his voice or altered his avuncular demeanour, but she got the distinct impression she'd just been 'bawled out'.

"*Kumasi* needs a shakedown plus the people of Earth need to see the latest example of what their tax credits are funding. You have three weeks to transit to Earth, show her off and on her return, have her running as smoothly as the proverbial Swiss watch." Commodore Axford paused to look her dead in the eye. "I also expect, by then, her captain to be a fully functioning, completely wholesome human being." Reclining slightly, he smiled broadly but it didn't quite make it to his eyes. "With that in mind, allow me to introduce you to a couple of your ship's complement."

He waved his hand to no one in particular. She had to resist the temptation to turn around as she heard the quiet hiss of the entrance to the OpsCen dilating open. A Lieutenant Commander from the Naval Medical Service and a marine Captain halted either side of her and saluted the Flag Officers. This time there was no resisting the temptation; her head, of its own volition, flick left then right to give both the once over before she'd realised it. A marine and a nurse: neither would be under her direct command. Nurses reported to the Surgeon General and the marine would, no doubt, be a member of an assault brigade; berthed but not stationed on the ship. With resentment swelling up at 'the situation' she was being manoeuvred into, she took an instant and intense dislike to both men. She couldn't see any way of avoiding what was coming.

Axford nodded in acknowledgement of their salutes. "Captain Magambál Talberg, allow me to introduce Lieutenant Commander Qamar Daeschner and Captain Sacha Kona, your partners 'for the purpose of cohabitation'. Gentleman, Captain Magambál Talberg." Again, he smiled, this time genuinely, like the wily old fox that he was. "Any Question?"

No subtext was necessary: '*Kumasi* will be *your* ship if you establish an intimate sexual relationship with these men. Obviously, you don't have to prostitute yourself; similarly, we don't have to give you command of the ship.' There were no questions.

Axford addressed her. "I'll be transferring my flag to *The Assegai* at eighteen hundred hours today then she'll be all yours. Have a safe and fulfilling voyage. Dismissed."

*****

She had completed her long anticipated first bridge inspection, which was about as satisfying as that ever so special celebratory meal where you lost your appetite just as you sat at the table. She'd also formally met her First Officer, Commander Naomi De La Haye. They had crossed paths before and De La Haye had greatly impressed her then. Her admiration for her second in command had taken a further fillip when she'd heard on the unofficial grapevine that De La Haye had turned down her own chance of a captaincy to serve on *Kumasi*.

Her First Officer had everything under control and competent individuals didn't appreciate being micromanaged, so she retired to her en-voyage cabin that was adjacent to the bridge. With the ship being prepped for departing space dock, a First Officer's responsibility, there wasn't really much for her to actually do. She skimmed the service records of a few of her junior offices - her command staff records had been scrutinised and inwardly digested long before any of them had set foot on *her* ship. Reflecting on the conversation with the Commodore; perversely, throughout the entire episode it was Admiral Akobundu-Tan, and her silence, that had been the most intimidating.

In truth, she was simply procrastinating, and it would be a couple of hours before she'd be needed on the bridge. When was the last time she had to consider contraception? More that five years certainly. She could narrow it down further if she devoted some thought to it. But that was just it, she didn't want to think about it because *it* was inextricably associated with *him* and she could do without the sorrow and ache in her heart just then. Like almost every single woman alive, her menstruation had been mitigated and regulated at two years after menarche and her getting regular periods. Medical intervention earlier than two years tended to have deleterious effects on later reproductive success. This mitigation was tailored to the individual and contingent on many genetic and physiological factors: in her case she had one, or occasionally two, periods every sixteen months or so.

Therein lies the rub: there were up to three stages during this cycle where one could still become pregnant. The largest single cause of unplanned pregnancies in the military was the woman losing track of these and simply failing to keep in mind that it was still possible for her to get pregnant. The second most common cause of unplanned pregnancies was the woman 'believing' the man when he told her he'd had reversable sperm attenuation treatment. There was really no excuse for any of this as contraception was so readily available, be it in drink, tablet, or infusion form. She called up a couple of the sleazier hologram sites for some 'inspiration'. After about ten minutes of viewing she was confident that she had a handle on polyandrous sex. Next, she tapped into the neural net to check that both Qamar and Sacha were still in her in-port cabin: the captain's in-port cabin was the most spacious living space on any spaceship so certainly big enough to accommodate three.

Calculating that a couple of hours ought to be more than enough time, she set off for the cabin to join her *companions*.

***

At the entrance to her in-port cabin she paused momentarily as it suddenly and rather belatedly occurred to her that, due to unimaginative assumptions, her research may have been incomplete. There appeared to be six basic combinations of sexual relations involving one woman and two men; anything else was simply a variation of those six. However, she'd only investigated the heterosexual male(s) to female, female to male(s) aspects. Clearly there could also be male to male scenarios which she'd overlooked. Deciding that the best course of action would be to improvise if any such male to male proceedings transpired, she entered.

10

Both men stopped what they were doing; Sacha unpacking and stashing, Qamar working at a consul that retracted back into the wall as soon as he stood. Neither man was standing at parade ground attention, but they weren't far off either. She took in the cabin with a single sweep; it had been configured pretty much as she would have arranged it to ergonomically accommodate three individuals. The only thing of note was the conspicuously oversized multi-occupants cocoon set vertically against the wall. Unsure of what do with some of her personal belongings, Sacha had placed them neatly to the side; exactly what she'd expect of a marine.

Clearly both men were selected so she'd find then attractive: very tall, slim, very dark and with a just hint of granite lurking behind their eyes. How, in God's name, did Rancid Roger know that this was the profile to entangle her? If this had been on Earth, she would have said that Qamar was from the Indian subcontinent and Sacha from Africa or, perhaps, the Middle East. She'd already tried, and been denied, access to their personnel records so she didn't even know which planets they were from. Yes, they were eye-catching but, giving the middle finger to Rancid Roger, she didn't have to like them.

She bit down the temptation to say, 'At ease,' and stepped fully into the four-metre by four-metre space: vastly roomy by spaceship standards but still a confined area. "There is no need for formality here, I expect us to use first names. So, Sacha, Qamar, I'm Magambál"

Neither man moved, relaxed, or spoke. "I have to be back on the bridge by fourteen thirty." Deciding that it would be a shame to clutter Sacha's handiwork she removed her tunic and placed it neatly over the back of the chair Qamar had risen from. When she started to undo her blouse, she'd expected them to move so that the cocoon aka 'bunk' could be lowered. But they both remain exactly where they were as if rooted. If the bunk wasn't lowered, then as far as she could gauge, only one of the six combinations would work. As she undid the last button, Qamar stepped up and stared down into her eyes.

"Personally, I don't much go for walking wankholes, Ma'am." Then he stepped past her and she heard the door hiss as it dilated and then contracted.

She was so taken aback by his actions that it took a while for his words to register. Before she could react, Sacha had taken a pace and was standing directly in front of her. Reaching out he unhurriedly started to refasten the buttons on her blouse and for the first time she understood why the buttons on blouses always seem to be the wrong way around; it was so that their sexual partner(s) could easily undress a woman.

"A little wine, some sweet lines and touch of romance, never goes amiss." With a warm smile, he looked down dreamily into her eyes. "I'm pretty sure the idea behind this bunkmates exchanging bodily fluids gig is that there are some things the captain of a really, really big ship like this ought to do simply because she really, really wants to and not because of 'duty'." He patted her on both shoulders, much as an elder sibling might do then stepped past. "I need to go check on my marines." Just as the door was contracting, he tossed back over his shoulder, "See you later, Blondie."

With the demise of the nation state and the migration from Earth accelerating the intermixing of races, very few people these days had blonde hair and even fewer still had red. Yes, she was exceedingly conspicuous, but no one had ever called her 'Blondie' before. If he hadn't worn 'that smile' and they weren't alone she wouldn't have recognised, and then accepted, it as a term of endearment…

Give her a cruiser with a crew in the tens of thousands and tell her to take point of an attack group and she'd relish the task. Ask her to engage in a personal relationship with a man and she really wouldn't have a clue where to begin. Such had been the state of affairs since puberty and as a bemused bystander she'd watched her contemporaries' brains being completely hijacked by their hormones. This behaviour was so unfathomable to her that she assumed that she must have been a lesbian. She now understood that, although caressing another woman's breasts had a lot going for it, she wasn't a lesbian, or for that matter bisexual, either. In the end, she concluded that it appeared she simply had far less appetite for carnal matters than the vast majority of her peers: which was perfectly fine by her because it enabled her to put her youthful energy and focus into more important things.

Rancid Roger: devious, underhand, manipulative, controlling and darn right conniving but not overtly callous. She'd been coerced - no, unsubtly and unashamedly blackmailed - into a relationship with two men: something she wasn't remotely emotionally equipped to deal with nor endowed with even the basic insights on how to manage. So presumably Sacha and Qamar had the way-with-all to cope with her; she was the captain of capital ship after all and it was *her* spiritual wellbeing that Rahumaehullah and Axford had carped on about.

It now seemed eminently sensible that for her next shot at congress she ought to approach the men individually. Engaging Sacha first would probably be the more prudent stratagem. In the interim she had a ship to shakedown. Slipping out of her dress uniform she donned the more ubiquitous work-a-day overalls and stepped into her ship boots with their built-in emergency maglocks.

***

The system checks were coming on apace, but the various ship-wide drills were being severely hampered by the thousand or so civilian technicians that were still aboard. The technicians were going to be a fixture for the next couple of weeks, at least, as myriad of inevitable glitches were ironed out. Ideally, she wanted to make their first superlight jump in the next six hours, but the civilians 'dawdled'. Jumping in twenty-four hours was looking more realistical and she needed to give her First Officer some elbow room. An impromptu captain's inspection was the order of the day.

The organisational structure on *her* ship was: along with the First Officer, the other executive officers, in decreasing seniority, were the department heads of ground support operations (GSO) - who was also her 3IC, weapons, engineering, navigation, homeostasis and operations. So, a canny move would be to show interest in a department whose head wasn't one of her execs: somewhere unfashionably parochial like transportation or logistics supply. Plumping for logistics she spent a leisurely two hours with her supply contingent, an enjoyable and informative duty she'd inexcusably failed to undertake after her first command, the corvette *Escalade*.

Equally illuminating was being present during the changing of the watch. Even with all tasks that could be accomplished by automatics being allocated to automatics, smaller vessels like Frigates, Corvettes and Fast Attack Crafts still had a ship's roster of six complete crews. When making the sequential superlight jumps of combat, four hours was about the maximum on duty personnel could 'stay one it' before they needed to be relieved. Larger ship, due to economies of scale, carried only five complete crews.

Everything about the inspection and her excursions around *her* ship was encouraging. A ship was like a living thing with, if not an actual personality then certainly each ship had, a distinct character. Antiquated European naval traditions or not, it will be with *Kumasi* that she will choose to bond, and that relationship will be her most significant relationship - she could already tell that she and her ship were going to get on famously.

***

It may have been her subconscious at work, but she doubted that - it was just coincidence. The most direct route from the second stowage depot, the location of her captain's inspection, to the bridge passed MedCen IV: Qamar's current location. This she knew because she'd had the prudent foresight to order continuous track reports on both men. Not because of anything as pathetic and emotional as insecurity but because 'if you can't measure and monitor, you can't manage' and she certainly needed to manage the circumstances she'd been strong-armed into. To be instantly updated on the whereabouts of either man, she simply had to think about it and the neural net would provide the answer

She was the captain of *this* ship and you don't flounce out on a captain. Having said that she wasn't certain that it was, in fact, 'the captain' Qamar had walked out on. Pausing at the entrance to MedCen IV she considered that, perhaps, she needed first to decide whether in this encounter she would be his captain or his...? His what? Perhaps this was the underlying issue? From her perspective, what exactly was the nature of the relationship other than the fact that it had been foisted on her? Now she'd stopped to analyse it, the answer was obvious: they were simply her gigolos and as such should pose no distractions to the running of *her* ship.

The arrangement of man-sized cubicles all the way up to the ceiling always reminded her of the honeycombed symmetry and uniformity of a beehive. An educated guess was that there was somewhere between seven hundred and a thousand of the empty compartments visible with probably another ten similar racks stacked behind these. To the left of the MedCen's entrance were a couple dozen booths with transparent partitions. The cubicles may have been empty, but all the booths were occupied by three individuals: a typical one doctor and two nurse combination. No doubt this was the medical teams also shaking down their systems.

She *knew* which booth Qamar occupied. Captains, and all executive officers, were linked via neural implants to the ship's command network that interconnected the bridge, major departments, and vital systems: giving them instant access to each other and mission critical information by simply thinking about it. Making directly for his cubical, she'd nearly covered half the hundred or so meters when she saw him rise from his console and walk through a hologram to begin writing on one of the transparent walls. The last time she'd witnessed something like that was during her preschool education; flabbergasted she stopped and looked on. He appeared to be drawing a diagram. Why didn't he use a hologram projector? Surely that was infinitely more precise and easier to accomplish.

While she puzzled this out a mischievous and somewhat unnerving idea slowly percolated into her consciousness. It underlined that she'd been presented with another, more troubling, enigma: she'd recognised Qamar at a distance *and* from behind. That she could tell it was him (back, shoulders and arse) meant, alarmingly, that some part of her awareness had been paying undue attention to those particular aspects of his physique. She suspected Rancid Rodger's Machiavellian hand at play, again. If that were the case then so be it, but no one could compel her to find someone desirable or make her feel affection!

When she entered the booth the doctor and the other nurse shot to their feet. "At ease." A captain was nothing if not a diplomat, she addressed the doctor. "Sorry to interrupt, but I wanted a quick word." She nodded at Qamar.

It would have been an exaggeration to say that the doctor and nurse saluted then bolted out of the cubicle, but not much of one. Taking a pace backwards to overly block his exit, she signalled just how dim a view she took on being walked out on. If he noted or was concerned by this it didn't show as he visibly relaxed, folded his arms and affably look down at her. Focussing on the drawing on the see-through panel behind him she pulled a questioning frown.

Keeping his gaze on her he answered, "It's a flow chart."

She knew that! Her frown changed from one of questioning to one of annoyance.

"Easier to follow in 2D." He didn't seem too bothered.

"A flowchart of what?"

"The causality's journey from battlefield to medical Jump Suites or icing. We lose a disproportionate number once on board; the weak link appears to be between triage and MedCen. The automated stretcher-bearers are given priority but, obviously, for those crucial minutes all therapeutic care is on hold."

"Then why not use the semi-intelligent medical units? They can administer treatment en route."

He smiled. "They're designed for combat situations planetside and though they often accompany the casualty up in the Hopper, their movement around a ship would be ponderous."

He was a Lieutenant Commander and outranked most of the doctors on *her* ship. "So, what would you recommend?" He smiled again, and, after the fact, she realised that she'd responded to him, and his explanation, as if he was one of her command staff.

"The automatics on the medical units are about fist sized and if fitted to an automated stretcher could continue to administer treatment." He paused, openly assessing her.

She wasn't accustomed to, or was amused by, assessments from subordinates. "And?"

"The convention is: once on-board ship, Saps make the calls. The combat surgeons and battlefield doctors are... reluctant. I've tried pointing out that, apart from triage or emergencies, it's been centuries since a surgeon actually made an incision but they're still not buying into it."

"I think your idea has merit and should be implemented with immediate effect."

"Captain, you're the captain of the ship." Again, he smiled, this time disarmingly "And although our automatics have a reliability and steadiness no human hand could manage, this is a still medical matter."

"You want me to let you fight you own battles?"

"Our 'relationship' is common knowledge all over the ship."

Rumours control; the most uncontainable force on any ship. And like all good captains she always ensured she was plugged-in: how wide the gap between speculations and reality? Which crews' concerns weren't reaching her by official channels? This was a brand-new ship with a brand-new crew, yet the gossip channels were already fully up to speed while she was behind the curve in identifying and recruiting 'reliable sources'. Having said that, although she'd determined that congress with Sacha was, on balance, the more prudent course of action, she felt she'd been presented with an unexpected opportune moment. "Speaking of our relationships, I think I have an unusually low libido."

"Why do you believe that?"

This was not the reaction she was expecting and felt put on her back foot. "Well, err... I've never been as interested in sex as any of my contemporaries... Make the partitions opaque."

"I will, when we're both ready." His 'tone' was superbly measured: assertive but just the right side of insolent. "What was your most fulfilling sexual experience?"

Again wrong-footed, she was instantly transported to a place she only visited when she deliberately and consciously chose to: recollections of the long deceased Second Lieutenant Sammi Corentin James Nishioka from the planet Ningu. They were crewmates on the Destroyer *Dumah Al Jandal* and she had loved him. He loved her and loved having sex with her - she would have supposed his fixation with her body obsessive if all the other junior offices weren't also frantically 'at it'. "It was with... we were close... I miss him." *'Pull yourself together.'* "But I don't miss having sex with him or anyone else for that matter."

Qamar nodded slowly, sympathetically. "Do you ever feel guilt or shame about having sex?"

It would be reasonable assumption that no one got to be a senior combat trauma nurse without matriculating in psychology. Having said that, no one got to be the captain of a ship without enduring never-ending psychological examinations and legions of psychometric profiling. "No." Ensuring her 'tone' was the non-Captain's she added, "The partitions are still transparent."

He did something with his eyebrows; she guessed that it might have something to do with being flirtatious but was stumped as to the appropriate response. Again, he flashed the eyebrow dance then said, "So what do you do to have fun?"

She'd *heard* of flirtation; she'd also *heard* of foreplay: this must be something to do with both. "I read and if I can find the time, I make it to the High-G gym..." She shrugged as she didn't know what else to say.

He grinned. "I didn't ask what you did to relax, I asked what you did for fun."

Fun? They'd been at war since just after her birth; captains of combat vessels didn't have *fun*. "Fun?!"

"How old were you when you decided you wanted to be a spaceship captain?"

"When I was six or, perhaps, seven-years-old. Why do you want to know that?"

"A determined, focussed, high-achiever that's been far too busy to have fun." He smiled and there was something almost predatory in the way he was looking down at her. He casually waved his hand as he languidly flopped into his seat and darkened the partitions. "Come sit on my lap, little girl," he susurrated. There was now nothing 'almost' about his predatory demeanour, yet she found herself taking hesitant steps towards him - it was 'almost' hypnotic the way she was being drawn. How were they going to achieve congress with her sitting on his lap? He'd asked her to sit there so presumably he knew.

He had her so enthralled that it almost precipitated an egregious schoolgirl error: one couldn't easily disconnect from the neural net. Her Exec team nearly started experiencing, vicariously, their captain becoming uncharacteristically erotically excited. She just managed to complete the mental switch to 'receive' as Qamar hungrily reached for her.

***

She was fully reintegrated into the ship's and Execs' comms and thus needed to keep a lid on it. Just as she likewise needed to resist the surprisingly strong urge to skip along the corridor. When was the last time she actually skipped? She couldn't remember but it must have certainly been pre-teens. Obviously, all this gaiety was not just the aftereffects of a gratifying sexual act but also of an emotional connection made. Despite her best efforts, she sensed that she was becoming... *fond* of Qamar. The flagrant and coldblooded manipulation by Rancid Roger that all military personnel were regularly subjected to, and the resulting brooding resentment they all felt, didn't seem to matter so much just then...

Oh, for God's sake, this was *her* ship!

Up ahead in the corridor, clearly waiting to buttonhole her was Admiral of the Fleet Akobundu-Tan and Commodore Axford. Did they know that she'd been...? Of course, they did - she'd just completed another of their bloody hamster-on-the-wheel trials! Whatever after sex delight she'd been feeling evaporated and she had to consciously stop herself from clenching and unclenching het fists as she approached them.

"Join us, Captain," Axford said, smiled and spun on his heels as soon as the Admiral had returned her salute. Arms behind back, he set off as if on a Sunday afternoon stroll. Standing next to her she was maybe five centimetres taller than the Admiral but even so there was something menacingly overawing about Akobundu-Tan and it had little to do with the braid on her epaulets. When she and the Admiral matched Axford's pace, he added, "This is a 3IC only briefing."

A Third in Command - Beyond Top Secret - Briefing; to be divulged only to her First and Second Officers. OK, they had her. She was intrigued. With an unknowable enemy, secrets could only be from their own personnel.

"I'm sure that, like all good captains, you've committed to memory the 3D blueprints of your ship so that you are completely familiar with it and its workings," the Commodore offered conversationally.

That went without saying, so why was he saying it? Matching them in their unconcerned perambulation she kept her lips tightly sealed. The trio turned left, down a corridor leading towards one of the mid deck messes - they were headed somewhere near the very centre of the ship.

With prepping for departure all corridor and access ways ought to have been bustling. This particular corridor was almost devoid of personnel, suspiciously so. Waiting until they had travelled some way down, she glanced behind and there, as expected, also ambling along about twenty-five metres behind them, were a couple of marine MPs - yet more personnel on *her* ship who were not *directly* under her command. Twenty-five metres ahead were another couple of marine MPs. She didn't let it bother her unduly, Admirals of the Fleet and Commodores, even when they ambled, did so with a purpose.

Near the end of the deserted corridor they came to a gradual halt. Looking around, there didn't appear to be anything significant about where they'd stopped. She guessed that was the point: her commanders were about to reveal something Most Secret about *her* ship. She'd pretend to be both surprised and impressed but even as the newly appointed captain of a corvette she'd heard that capital ships had 'Most Secret', concealed, heavily shielded secondary command centres. Engines down, life support down, as long as weapons functioned, capital ships kept fighting. She, and the vessels she'd commanded to date, wouldn't have survived the engagements they had if capital ships hadn't sacrificed themselves in valiant rear-guard action - it's what they do!

Commodore Axford glanced up and down the corridor then grinned at her. "Do you know a memorable magical phrase like 'Abracadabra' or Open Sesame' that you'd like to share?"

"Fejétől bűzlik a hal, Sir."

Axford raised an eyebrow. "Meaning?"

"It's central European, similar to 'abracadabra', Sir."

"Then say the magic words, Captain."

"Fejétől bűzlik a hal!"

The bulkhead they were standing next to hissed then dilated open... OK, that was impressive: you could have walked past a thousand times and never guessed it was a door. And there wasn't even a hint of this aperture on any schematics she'd seen.

"Let's go into the enchanted cave then shall we, children?" The Commodore waved her in.

Stepping forward, what she expected to enter was a ComCen in trickle-power mode - masking it from the ship's internal sensors: what she actually stepped into was just another brightly lit corridor. As the door hissed closed behind them, she couldn't help feeling that she'd moved into a ship within a ship, but there was more to the feeling than that. In the space services, you quickly developed a sixth sense of just how crammed the ship you were aboard was - a kind of subconscious density meter. That sense was telling her that this 'area' wasn't just a ship within a ship; it was excessive redundant space within *her* very overcrowded ship. Now she was totally unnerved by Axford's frivolousness and Akobundu-Tan's silence.

"It's Hungarian, an old European language: literally, 'Fish stinks from its head'," the Admiral informed the Commodore.

And Magambál nearly jumped out of her skin.

Smiling the Commodore nodded in acceptance of the Admirals' titbit then set off down an equally deserted corridor. So, it appeared that the Commodore knew their destination and the Admiral was along for the ride. Speaking of the Admiral: having sneaked a quick glance, she remained so stony-faced that Magambál was fairly sure the Military Operations Quadrant Commander was trying her damnedest not to laugh. As if to confirm, the Admiral looked up, askance, at her.

"Though ostensibly heterosexual, in some indices on the spectrum you are borderline male-brain, Captain." The Admiral paused to let her mull that over. "Particularly in personifying the ship you command," she paused for a second time to let that sink in. "You probably stop short of thinking of it as a *he* or a *she*, as most male captains do, but you do have *feelings* towards your ship. And that is extremely unhealthy in a woman who hold tens of thousands of lives in her hands."

Magambál opened her mouth to, well, not argue but to at least offer an opposing perspective but Akobundu-Tan cut her off. "You are about to be welcomed into the big-league, Captain. You wouldn't be here if you hadn't earned your place. Nevertheless, the stakes are much higher, so the rules are different." She hadn't realised that the Admiral was being conversational until the *Boss* altered her tone to 'directive'. "Your ship is a machine, an inanimate object: the motivational drives and needs that should be directed towards sex and reproduction *need* to be directed towards sexual and reproductive acts."

Yes, she was taking on board everything the Admiral said but the thing that was quietly incensing her was this vast unoccupied space on *her* ship; they had covered over fifty metres and not encountered a single soul. When they approached a standard bulkhead door it opened automatically. On entering Magambál saw that it was a briefing room but an exceedingly small, or perhaps more appropriately, intimate, briefing room. Already present were three Guardsman, lounging around, who immediately shot to their feet. Guardsman? Something to do with specialist infantry, always sky-blue suited, always wearing sunglasses. Grunts!

"At ease," the Admiral commanded as she strolled up to them. One of the Guardsman, the male, was easily over two metres tall and the Admiral made it to just past his waist - an almost comical sight. Turning to face her, Akobundu-Tan fixed her with a cold, hard stare. Magambál felt the hairs on the back of her neck bristle. "These are *my* strategic assets stationed on *your* ship."

She would have begun to feel foolish at being a little scared, but she sensed that Axford was also mesmerised.

"They are on your ship because they have earned some 'down time'. I could have simply sent you a brief about them, but some things are best done up close and personal." The Admiral smiled wickedly then gave all her attention to the tall Guardsman. "For the benefit of the captain, are you married to both these women?"

"Yes, Ma'am."

"Do you love them both and equally?"

"Yes, Ma'am."

"Basche, your insights re the Bulges' intra-atmosphere craft and mutual detection of movement have proved invaluable." Smoothly pivoting at the waist, she turned her attention to the two women. "And you two, do you now *believe* that your husband is extraordinarily lucky?"

"Yes, we do, Ma'am," the sky-blue clad women answered in unison.

Tuning fully to face her, as if to gauge her reaction, Akobundu-Tan folded her arms then said, "Love and luck are not usually associated with a military campaign… OK, shades off."

All three Guardsman took off their sunglasses and she instantly noted that both women had cybernetic eyes. Were they lost in combat or had they been deliberately implanted to enhance vision? *You brought me all the way here to show me artificial eyes? No. So, what am I supposed to be seeing...?* She had no recollection of ever seeing a Guardsman without sunglasses. The sunglasses were to 'conceal' the cybernetic eyes. Why conceal them? The man, the husband, had normal eyes, so...? An Admiral of the Fleet was personally briefing her on this, so...?

Patience running perilously low, Magambál badly needed to short circuit this peekaboo nonsense without delay: stepping forward she reached out to place the back of her hand on one of the women's cheeks. That was disappointing - the woman's cheek felt warm to the touch. If she wasn't being presented with life-like robots, what was it? Momentarily switching her attention to the man, she concluded that, apart from being rather tall, there was nothing exceptional there... Strategic assets? What was the primary mission of the Guardsman? Racking her brains only led to some vague recollection of notions about 'reconnaissance'. Before she was fully aware that she had, she'd already succumbed and given the Admiral an 'I give in' shrug.

Still locking eyes with her the Admiral raised an eyebrow then abruptly demanded, "Thariyan, how would you describe yourself?"

The darker skinned of the two women answered, "Loosely, I'd describe myself as a woman. If one wanted to be more pedantic about it, I'd define myself as a sentient silicone-based life form, Ma'am."

And for the second time in minutes Magambál nearly jumped out of her skin. "You're a robot?!"

"We prefer the term 'android', Ma'am."

Could a robot, even one with body temperature warm skin, have any say in what it's called?

"Do you know what a blunderbuss is, Captain?" The Admiral casually asked.

She nodded.

"That's *Kumasi*. But from time to time I may also require finesse; any well-stocked toolbox also contains precision instruments. Those are the Guardsman and Stingers - *my* laser scalpels. De La Haye, your 2IC, already knows about the Guardsman and that these are stationed onboard, she was 3IC on…" She turned to the Commodore.

"*Texarkana*."

"… the *Texarkana*. Why am I telling you this?" Again, the Admiral pause to coldly lock eyed with her. "That borderline male brain of yours is the reason I'm here to personally brief you about the Guardsman corps. The thing most pertinent to this particular discussion is this: it appears that swinging dicks aren't overly fussy about the holes they pop themselves in to, even android ones. On the other hand, through trial and innumerable errors, we now know that organic holes are universally fastidious about which swinging dicks they get it together with, especially pertaining to anything long-term. The holes are happy to play with toys of course, but, and it has nothing to do with sexuality, there is no 'bonding' with the inorganic. There are no 'women' Guardsman." Akobundu-Tan then paused, adding weight to her words.

"With AIs, quantum computers, neural nets, and the vast array of technology available to them, there are some captains who, even when we factor in their strategic and tactical brilliance, are statistical outliers. Or, to put it another way, extraordinarily lucky. Personally, I like these extraordinarily lucky captains commanding my capital ships. And over the years I've come to realise that that a happy ship's captain is a lucky ship's captain… You were looking happy earlier; energised, positively beaming. Were you happy, Captain?"

Captains of dreadnoughts didn't usually blush like embarrassed schoolgirls, but she could feel herself redden.

"*Kumasi* will be one of the spear points of my planetary assaults and you, Captain Talberg, are its commander. I want you lucky - stop anthropomorphising this ship - get it on with Sacha!"

Magambál wasn't an ardent believer in the semi-mystical 'metaphysical explanation' but she wasn't a vehement detractor either. Just like with the 'intelligent beings' v. 'natural phenomenon' debate about the nature of the Bulges, she naturally gravitated towards the middle ground. Love, luck, and warfare? An inner voice wanted to ridicule such dissonance while another voice observed that the nominal outsider 'love' was in fact a prerequisite in many conflicts: 'love of the cause' by the True Believer. So, the point of her emotional disconnect seemed to be the idea of 'romantic love' and combat. She nodded in acceptance of the Admiral's *directive*.

"How many Guardsman units are stationed on…" she supressed the urge to say *my* "…this ship, Ma'am?"

"Four to six three-man teams are usually ensconced on a ship this size but for this mission you'll only have this merry bunch."

"Though Guardsman are not free to intermingle with the ship's personnel there is another of the Admiral's strategic assets on board who, with the usual caveats, will be at liberty to do so," Commodore Axford stated; then after she raised a questioning eyebrow added, "He's Platinum Stinger."

As the captain, she wasn't engaged in a 'conversation' with her superiors and took it as a compliment that she was being informed about this posting in the first place.

"Enjoy your R & R: use the time to get some real depth to your relationship," the Admiral advised the three Guardsman and made as if ready to depart but then spun and fixed her with a riveting stare. "And you know what you have to do - *Kumasi* is 'machine'!"

As she followed the Admiral and Commodore out of the boutique briefing room, she wondered at the cost of building one life-like robot? In any computation involving military expenditure Magambál's unit of currency was 'the cost of building a squadron of Ground Support Fighters'. Some intuition suggested that the cost of each would be several such units. How many of them were there in total? A robot could be programmed to imitate/emulate love, but you couldn't do that to a person… or could you? Rancid Roger certainly had other ideas - the Guardsman affirmed that he loved both his wives. In less than twenty-four hours she was beginning to 'like' Qamar…

Rancid Roger was good, but he wasn't *that* good, and she'd prove it.

Chapter 2

Superficially *Kumasi* looked radically different to any other capital ship in the fleet: from a distance *he* resembled an enormous duckbill. Being the first cruiser to be launched after the battle of the Omega Zero system he'd had a thermo-ceramic outer shell grafted on like an epidermis layer. The carapace offered negligible additional protection, but it made him streamlined and thus highly capable of intra-atmosphere operations. It added only three percent to the ship's mass and now, just like an ancient galleon, he had ports through which he brought his weapons to bear; unlike an ancient galleon's his took microseconds to open.

Magambál scanned the entirety of *her* already proficiently operating bridge/OpsCen then slowly sat back in her reclined couch and coolly said, "Cast off, Number One!"

While De La Haye promptly replied, "Aye aye Ma'am. Cast off!" Magambál was pretty sure that Polynesians didn't say 'cast off' when launching their ships - so much for non-European naval traditions. The superstructure reverberated with the pinging of thousands of umbilicals being detached and gangways disengaging; *Kumasi* eased away from the habitat *Mystery Landing*. Although ships were constructed in shipyards around Earth's and Saturn's moons and the planets Trolus, Bacci and Janneri, because of the incredibly high attrition of the war, vessels were only completed to the point of being able to travel super-light. Then, with a skeleton crew of civilians, they were flown to a habitat in a combat zone.

These military habitats, colloquially known as 'death stars', were mobile factories that then 'weaponised' the ships. On her first tour as a midshipman she's assumed that military habitats earned this nomenclature because this was where a ship's main armament was installed. That assumption had proven erroneous; apparently, the term had evolved from some other cultural reference the origin of which she was unable to glean.

The mini-world habitats were the logical result of another pre-super-light travel fallacy going up in smoke - terraforming. It proved far too difficult and costly in terms of both money and energy to try and terraform a planet or moon that hosted an ecosystem. Battling the innumerable trillions of organisms symbiotically keeping it in its original state of equilibrium to effect a permanent change, to a human-friendly ecosystem, was nigh impossible. Of course, seeding a barren body was a far less expensive option but as a millennial undertaking, in human timescales, impractical. In the final analysis it was so much more efficient and effective to simply build a mini-moon from scratch or co-opt a suitable asteroid: with the added boon that you could strap on a propulsion system and move it, all-be-it infrequently, around.

Clearly the bioadapted did not faced the same handicaps but even they had limits. After all, the basic human chassis could only be modified so far. The genetically in-built glass ceiling being slightly less than the maximum mammalian diversity on Earth. Splicing genetic code from other vertebrate branches, say reptilian, never led to viable zygotes for some unknown reason. In the end the bioadapted were only able to colonise six of the so far discovered planets whose ecosystems had been just too marginal for the non-bioadapted - actually, it was two planets and four moons.

We have thirty-seven planets, they have six. We are numbered in the tens of billions, they in the tens of thousands. *And* we know where they were. If 'the hybridisation problem' had come to a shooting war, it would have been one-sided. The bioadapts have assumed, not unreasonably, that we are too preoccupied with the Bulges to bother with them. If they were smart, they'd use this time wisely because, from their perspective, 'the hybridisation problem' was only in abeyance.

In reality there was no 'hybridisation problem'. The same gene editing that could endow a foetus's blood with the capacity to carry the same oxygen load as sperm whale, could also ensure that said foetus was sterile… Auto-sterilisation could be, and was, embedded in *all* bioadapted gene editing apparatus. Just like that, it was slipped in when they weren't looking. Magambál only knew about this ultra-high classified information because as a young lieutenant she'd been on a covert mission to 'disable' cloning equipment on one of the bioadapted worlds. Gene editing was relatively simple, cloning something as complex as a human was another ball game and required *technology* - the bioadapts didn't know it, yet, but they were a dying breed.

Kumasi was now clear of the habitat. "Set nine-jump course for Earth, Number One."

"Aye aye, Ma'am."

Theoretically they could've made Earth in a single jump taking about thirteen hours ship time. However, twelve of those hours would have to be spent in a Jump Suite. That would have rendered the crew beyond ineffectual after the jump. The recovery period after a drop back to normal spacetime like that would take at least four to five hours. A three jump, circa forty-two hours ship time, transit would have been the minimum militarily expedient voyage. But they weren't being military expedient, this was a shakedown - they'd arrive at the Sol system in about a week.

"Lock down! Lock down! Jump in three minutes!"

And that shakedown began right now! None of that of that slack five-minute jump warning here. They had just cast off and anyone, even a civilian, who hadn't anticipated a jump didn't deserve to be on *her* ship. Leisurely scanning around her bridge she noted that everything was running as proficiently as her very high standards demanded. It was gratifying to conclude that De La Haye had similar exacting standards. Magambál made a mental note to compliment her First Office on this.

"Lock down! Lock down! Jump in two minutes!"

The first jump would be a simple twenty-two lightyear hop: coming to a complete stop for a deep-dive analysis, and ironing out the bugs, of all non-weapons systems and automatics. Weapons would be tested in later jumps when they'd locate a suitable planetoid to permanently disfigure…

"Homeostasis reports a ship-wide estimate that as many as fifteen personnel may not make it to a Suite in time. Shall we abort jump, Ma'am?" De La Haye calmly announced on the super discrete 2IC, 3IC net.

Flicking a casual glance at the First Officer confirmed that none of the bridge complement could even guess that they were communicating. It was in the best interest of crew and ship that *any* second in command 'check out' *any* new captain - it's what she'd do. Abort jump indeed! *"Homeostasis to alert post-jump medical teams in the relevant sectors. Continue countdown,"* she replied with equal calm.

"Lock down! Lock down! Jump in ninety seconds!"

Kumasi was a heavy cruiser - a combat vessel - not a leisure craft: as many as fifteen personnel were about to learn the excruciatingly painful and potentially fatal lesson of not dawdling on her ship! Just as well that the medical teams also needed shaking-down then. The couch auto-strapped her in and she slipped on her face mask.

"Lock down! Lock down! Jump in sixty seconds!"

The lighting in the OpsCen dimmed and shifted to red. The holograms above her reclined position showed 'green across the board' - her ship was checked and ready for the jump. She could feel just how eager he was as his enormous superlight engines began to spool-up.

"Lock down! Lock down! Jump in thirty seconds!"

The biocontainment shield fell across her like a steel blanket pressing her firmly into the couch and the artificial gravity cut out.

"Lock down! Lock down! Jump in ten seconds."

Her vision bleared as her surroundings seemed to become momentarily insubstantial. Next, came the nerve-shattering, teeth-chattering vibrations, as if she were being peeled from the inside out. Unlike most, she actually understood the mathematics behind superlight jumps; not that she could explain it to a six-year-old. The superlight engines were flooding every molecule, atom, and quark on and in the ship with bright neutrinos. With this almost instantaneous over-production of energy, any surplus was dumped via a lattice imbedded in its exterior; causing the ship to pulsate in the infrared and visible EM spectrum. When the ship's entireness was supersaturated, those very same bright neutrinos would be 'persuaded' they were someplace else - in this instance, someplace twenty-two lightyears distant.

It took the bright neutrinos a finite length of time to 'decide' that, yes, they were in this new location: ship jump time. The longer the jump the longer the 'indecision'. Once settled in the new location, hey presto, the bright neutrinos discover that they are 'attended' by all those same molecules, atoms, and quarks. Ships 'flashed' when they re-entered normal spacetime, releasing the final gasp of excess energy from the superlight drives. There had to be at least a thirty percent surfeit of energy from the drives for a safe jump because if there was a shortfall the ship would 'leave' spacetime but wouldn't rematerialise.

Organic matter, especially nervous systems, respond exceptionally poorly to 'the period of indecision' AKA ship jump time. Cells structures began a rapid and accelerating disintegration as the electrostatic bonds in the atoms of organic molecules that bind the nucleolus, chromatin, ribosomes, and mitochondrion etc. slacken. The biocontainment shield that mitigated the most damaging and debilitating aspects of this was in fact a superimposition of a combination of fields: a multi-layered electric field from the cellular level outwards, enclosed in super-dense, body-hugging gravity field.

Hence the apparent massive increase in weight and the ship's artificial gravity cessation. Each couch in a Jump Suite was a mini multi-field generator.

Not strapped to a couch and enclosed in a biocontainment shield during a jump? In a very literal sense, you began to fall to pieces at the atomic level. This physical phenomenon caused every pain receptor in the human body to send a message of overstimulation that the brain interpreted as unremitting excruciating agony. Tardy enough to not make it to a Suite at all? If the irreversible cellular damage didn't immediately get you then the inevitable mental breakdown triggered by a hyper-accelerated Alzheimer's did. Still... the prevention was almost as unpleasant as the illness.

"Biocontainment shielding up! Stand by for one G in five... four... three... two... one! Lock down over! Jump medical teams to Sector three, deck seven and Sector seven, deck eleven."

The standard post-jump passive sensor sweeps showed everything in the green answering some basic questions like; are we where we're supposed to be, are the any threats either natural or artificial etc?

"Full active sweep, Number One."

"Aye aye, full active sweep, Ma'am," De La Haye promptly replied.

Medical teams to only two Sectors would suggest that the tardy fifteen had been in two groups - most likely civilian technicians. Ship jump time had been in minutes so although agonising, probably no permanent damage. She'd get the details in her daily Captain's briefing. "Engineering, report!"

"All systems operating within parameters. Propulsion eight-four percent efficient, we'll start dialling that up immediately and be in the high nineties by Earth-fall, Ma'am." That her response had been almost instantaneous and conveyed over the command neural net spoke volumes to the efficiency of the Engineering Officer of the Watch, Lieutenant Thi Thuy. What was a captain going to demand post-jump - get ahead of the curve! Magambál supressed a smile.

"Ship-wide life support systems set and stable; artificial gravity intermittent on deck seven and has been disabled." Homeostasis also reported over the neural net.

"Active sweep completed: no external threats, situation normal, Ma'am." De La Haye reported.

Nor had anyone on *her* bridge puked - after-jump recovery was also another good indicator of a crew's efficiency. Every section and system on the ship needed to function as proficiently has her bridge crew. By the time they reached Earth she'd have the entire ship operating up to her extremely high standards... Time to get out of her deputy's hair. She slid out of the couch and stood. "Number One, you have the bridge."

"Aye aye, Ma'am.

***

She entered her in-port cabin to find Sacha sitting at the consul with his back to the door, clearly engrossed in something, and immediately noticed that his right arm was in a medical brace. He was right-handed - she wasn't even going to try and theorise on how she'd picked up on this, but he was - so the brace was a significant but not totally debilitating impediment.

Turning to face her he smiled then said, "Just checking to see who'd turned up." She raised an eyebrow, so still grinning, he added, "Blondie or the very serious and very focused Captain."

Her purpose for retiring to her in-port cabin, as opposed to her en-voyage cabin, was to signal to her 2IC that she'd seen enough and was totally satisfied with OpsCen. Between the two of them they needed to start shaking down the rest of the ship, beginning with Homeostasis - fluctuating artificial gravity indeed! That had been her intention but something about Sasha's boyishness... Mind you, he'd obviously sustained a serious injury. "What happened to your arm?"

He looked down at his arm disdainfully. "This? This is what you get for having a full Marine assault battalion on a ship that's *not* on a combat mission - gotta keep the boys and girls busy. Suit-free high G fire and manoeuvre exercise."

A status report of additional power usage in one of the Sectors, Sector nineteen, deck eleven if memory served her right, surfaced in her mind. "I see." She was about to ask, 'how he was feeing' but suspected that was a tad too 'Captain'. Personal situations weren't really her forte but the warmth she had with Qamar gave her sense of how to be informal and familiar. "What I think I'm hearing is that some make-work high G nonsense means I'll have to be gentle with you."

Frowning and feigning hurt feelings he flexed the damaged arm a few times, as if pumping iron then proclaimed, "This is a thought-controlled nanoparticle drug delivery orthosis splint. You see, unlike space-bound types, us marines need to keep fighting even when gravely wounded."

"What I think I'm hearing is someone saying they're good to go."

"How many blonde women do you think I've ever seen in my entire life? Even if I were laid-out on an automated stretcher, I'd still be good to go." His smile widened as he stood and reached her in one pace. With his hands under her armpits, he effortlessly lifted her off her feet into a passionate kiss.

***

A good thirty-five percent of a ship's power output was allocated to keeping the crew alive and functioning with militarily proficiency - homeostasis. Lieutenant Commander Thorn wasn't exactly quaking in his maglock boots, but he was obviously finding a no-notice inspection from both Captain and First Officer rather unnerving.

"Well, er, we've traced the fault to the superconducting cabling along deck seven, er, Ma'am. But haven't yet ascertained whether it's the cables themselves or the cryogenic systems."

In this instance Magambál thought it best if she left the chivvying along to her First Officer and as De La Haye opened her mouth

Thorn quickly added, "We'll have one G restored within eight hours, Ma'am,

"We jump in four hours, Lieutenant Commander." Even the most benign interpretation of De La Haye's tone would have said 'admonition'.

Thorn shifted his weight form one foot to the other then back again. "We'll do our best to turn it around by then, Ma'am."

A chain was only as strong as its weakest link - Magambál wondered if she was looking at her weakest link. 'Do our best' attitude wasn't the 'get it done' that she expected on *her* ship...

De La Haye smiled warmly at the Lieutenant Commander. "I glad to hear that, Lieutenant Commander."

The man visibly relaxed and Magambál speculated that she'd have De La Haye's recommendation on his reassignment within an hour. It wasn't only the ship's systems that needed shaking down, some people looked good on a dossier but... She *heard* a subtle beep in her left ear that was in reality a message projected directly into her brain via the command neural net. Then she *heard* the message: '*Warning Order. Retask. Weapons test and ready to move soonest.*' Though the message was aural it could have been an image or taken any other sensory form and its arrival and delivery as it had, without her consent, could only have been sent from C in C of the ninth fleet, Admiral of the Fleet Rahumaehullah.

She calmly drew a breath and waited, that had only been the attention getter. '*Enemy activity detected in the Rancia sector, near enough to cause concern but not close enough to attract its protective fleet. Mission: investigate and report.*' No doubt coded files were also being simultaneously downloaded into *Kumasi's* NavComs.

A scouting mission for a heavy cruiser, albeit one that wasn't yet combat ready? Hardly. She was being asked to have a 'look' and if expedient, 'shoot'. '*Mission: investigate and report,*' she confirmed her orders.

'*Set condition SQ2. Jump in T minus one hour for weapon test,*' she ordered over the command neural net. They both turned to her; De La Haye in anticipation, Thorn in trepidation.

"We, well ah, one hour, we won't be able to…"

"Do your best Lieutenant Commander," she cut him off and spun on her heels. The man had to go but right now she had bigger fish to fry.

"Set condition SQ2! Jump in T minus one hour!" Blared over the tannoy.

De La Haye caught up with her in a couple of paces, then with a sense of satisfaction they both received sequentially the affirmation of her orders and confirmations of 'will be ready for jump' from her other department heads over the neural net. With a thought she 'read in', verbatim, her 2IC and 3IC on the retasking from fleet C in C.

'I'll go assist weps,' Lieutenant Commander Edzai Stromme, her 3IC, proposed in response.

She gave her assent. This was the level of initiative she expected from her Execs: ground support operations (GSO) didn't need its head for this weapon firing, but the weapons team would be overstretched.

"And I'll go see if we can squeeze more out of the engines before the jump, Ma'am," De La Haye declared. She nodded in agreement then her 2IC added, "I'll have him reassigned to somewhere less challenging."

Magambál paused as if considering this. "Let's give him until the live firing to redeem himself. I'll be in my en-voyage cabin." Balance! If her First Officer had a 'stick' inclination then, as Captain, she needed to sway towards 'carrot'. She didn't need to explain that she was retiring to her en-voyage cabin to get, from fleet C in C, the meat to put on the bones of their orders.

***

The last thing she'd expected was to be involved in a four-way conversation. The hologram of Admiral of the Fleet Rahumaehullah - to be expected, he was fleet C in C. Commodore Axford's? Possibly, as she was one of his directly reports. But Admiral of the Fleet Akobundu-Tan's? That required some explaining; not that she, a mere captain, would be given one. Was Rahumaehullah being micromanaged by Akobundu-Tan? Hardly.

Akobundu-Tan looked her up and down as if she was physically present then she kicked off the briefing, "I now sense a general satisfaction and contentment, that I look for in all my senior commanders, about you, Captain."

How was one supposed to respond to a remark like that?

Akobundu-Tan nodded to Rahumaehullah who without preamble started, "As a rule the Bulges never deployed forces that we, in the most liberal sense of the words, would consider reconnaissance or scouts; as we've seen on innumerable occasions, they tend to emerge en masse and spoiling for a fight. So, this Rancia detection of approximately seven of their ships would appear to be somewhat atypical."

The hologram burst into life above her desk displaying the schematic of an unremarkable solar system. The seven symbols representing the enemy's mega-ships were positioned in the plane and about halfway between the system's scattered disk and outermost gas giant planet. Not somewhere you'd find much in the way of anything except an occasional exceptionally rare comet. The ships appeared to be stationary, something Magambál had never witnessed. She glanced at the time stamp - thirteen hours fifty minutes time lag. This information was from long-range sensors so only moderate fidelity, she reappraised; the handful of enemy ships weren't moving very fast.

"I take it you're up to speed on the latest theory about the Bulges?" Rahumaehullah asked.

The Shadow Puppets Hypothesis postulating that: 1) baryonic matter (us - and everything we can see, feel, detect) accounts for a mere five percent of the total mass of the universe. Gravity and bright neutrinos make-up about eighty-eight percent, which leaves a missing seven percent, or so; 2) what we perceive as the Bulges were simply sophisticated amalgamated baryonic matter drones, controlled via projected bright neutrinos and 'gravity beams'; 3) this projection technology was operated by MMB's - Missing Matter Beings (them);

4) the MMB's were significantly more technologically advanced than us; 5) the MMB's could be thought of as being from a parallel universe but not really because - and this is the really crucial bit from a how to defeat them perspective - we were both bound by the same laws of physics.

Personally, she didn't have a strong view regarding this particular yarn vis-á-vis any other outlandish conjecture on the nature of the Bulges. In fact, she was inclined to deem the concept that, in the Milky Way Galaxy, there were corresponding missing matter stars, missing matter solar systems and missing matter 'beings', as being just about on the ragged edge of plausibility. Gravity beams on the other hand were, however, a bit of a stretch. The science laughed at the idea: gravity was simultaneously the weakest and, on interstellar scales, the strongest of the fundamental forces; after centuries of trying, no one had even got close to quantising it.

She nodded in confirmation and Rahumaehullah continued, "A reasonable assumption, which is borne out by the stupendous oversufficiency in their energy use, is that this 'projecting' is staggeringly inefficient and inaccurate. So, sooner or later they, just as we would in their place, try to manifest themselves physically in our baryonic realm. It's also reasonable to assume that in any such crossover they'd do/manifest something we had not seen before - we've never witnessed only seven ships in formation before nor have we ever encountered any of their ships at low velocity." The Admiral paused for a glance and an unspoken meeting of minds with his boss before continuing, "You're the nearest ship with any credible capability; go have a looksee and report."

"If this is them dipping their toe in the waters, let's disabuse them of the habit," Akobundu-Tan appended with a delicate wave of her hand.

Not for the first time, it occurred to Magambál that there was something difficult to define but definitely 'there' that was chillingly lethal about Admiral of the Fleet Akobundu-Tan; she nodded assent.

"You'll have all updates, real-time. I have the flotilla on thirty minutes readiness, so if there are any gate-crashers or things become wildly interesting, we can be on station in under eleven hours. Any questions?" Commodore Axford asked in a tone that suggested that there shouldn't be.

"No, Sir."

<h1 align="center">Chapter 3</h1>

A suitable target had been identified; a rouge planet long ago ejected from its home solar system that was roughly the size of Jupiter's moon, Ganymede. It had no atmosphere and no local star, so therefore extremely unlikely to harbour, or ever evolve, life. No point in messing around, they were going to go about this as if it were a combat drop into contact.

'Biocontainment shielding up! Stand by for one G in five... four... three... two... one! Lock down over! Weapons free!'

All OpsCen personnel were suited and booted in full combat armour and strapped into their couch. No verbal reports this time; all the relevant information she needed swirled above her. It took her a few seconds to focus in on the holograms - everything in the green... except... deck seven's artificial gravity. Dammit! The drop had been calculated to bring them sweeping past the target's equator at fifteen thousand kilometres to port and they were right on the money.

"Bring railguns sixteen through twenty-seven online and lock in on target." *Kumasi* possessed over two hundred railguns but no need to be profligate.

"Railguns sixteen through twenty-seven locked on."

Railguns were simple kinetic, and primarily ship-to-ship, weapons. The depleted uranium shells, travelling at 0.69 light speed, would penetrate shields, puncture ships (even Bulges' ones) on one side, tear through interiors shattering all in their paths, exiting the opposite sides. What would they do to the naked surface of a planet without an atmosphere to dissipate the projectile's energy? "Fire at will and stand by to reverse heading for a missile and laser pass."

Magambál focussed on the hologrammatic readouts as they displayed the salvo's effects... OK, she'd not expected that: volcanic eruptions ejecting magma tens of kilometres high at the points of impacts and oscillations along the mantle as if it was momentarily liquid and this side of the planet was one gigantic turbulent ocean.

"Reverse heading and fire at will!"

"Reversing heading!"

Smoothly, she'd almost go as far as saying elegantly, the helmsman brought the ship about. *Kumasi's* superstructure reverberated with launch of the missiles. This time the lasers and missile strikes were far less dramatic, they didn't even register in the visible spectrum. This was mainly because the dual pulse laser fire was set to low power, and the missiles warheads were blanks. Yet it was a sobering thought to note: even if she'd fired all missiles armed with the plethora of warheads available (HE, fusion, fusion, antimatter, etc), discharged the full complement of lasers at full power and emptied every armoury on *Kumasi* all she'd achieve would be to scar the diminutive planet. The Bulges had completely disintegrated Omega Zero Three...

Everything was still in the green and all responses had been within the parameters she'd expect on *her* ship, except, of course, that vexing matter of homeostasis. "All stations stand down and resume normal operations. Prepare for live combat jump in half an hour."

While her orders were being 'read back' a text message flashed in her visual cortex via the command neural net. It was De La Haye's recommendation that Thorn be replaced by his deputy, Lieutenant Cinthia Ghanashyam. Ghanashyam hadn't made it on to her 'need to get to know' list and had she chosen to, Magambál could have instant access to her service record and much else besides. Yet this was a recommendation from a 2IC and unless there are compelling reasons to differ, it was considered bad form for a captain to overlook any such recommendations - it also put unnecessary strain on a ship's pivotal command relationship.

She replied her concurrence via the command neural net. Ghanashyam would now be informed of her new responsibilities (promotion would come later, on satisfactory performance) and 'read in' on the command neural net. If she was the woman for the task, as De La Haye had implied, she ought not to have been surprised by her advancement: an entire deck's A/G being U/S was intolerable on any military vessel. As for Thorn, he'd be redeployed to head a section (as opposed to a department head) somewhere in engineering. An organogram of her reorganised Exec registered briefly in her visual cortex which, as captain, she authorised and formally recorded...

"Lock down! Lock down! Combat jump in three minutes!"

Half an hour had flown by and her ship wasn't as tight she'd ideally like it, but it was as tight as it was ever going to be for this jump into the unknown. They would drop about eight light-hours distance from the Bulges with the objective being to conduct a minimum of twenty-four hours of passive scanning or until a 'significant event'.

"Lock down! Lock down! Combat jump in two minutes!"

Rahumaehullah had speculated that the seven Bulge ships was an attempt by them to transition over to 'our side'. A familiar tingle in the pit of her stomach alluded to something more extraordinary about to unfold. Her brain translated this 'tingle' into a simple phrase - a trap!

"Lock down! Lock down! Combat jump in ninety seconds!"

The concept of a trap implied purpose/agency in the human sense and that was certainly something the Bulges had never displayed. Still 'trap' was what she *sensed*.

"Lock down! Lock down! Combat jump in sixty seconds!"

Trap or no trap, she had always been at the sharp end but had never lost a ship. Badly damaged, often. Debilitated, on occasions. Disabled yes, but never destroyed. And she wasn't about to start now.

"Lock down! Lock down! Combat jump in thirty seconds!"

She wouldn't go as far as to say that she was a believer in 'fate.' But she didn't exactly disbelieve either. Despite her agnosticism she couldn't help feeling that there was something… fitting that this was hers and *Kumasi* mission.

"Lock down! Lock down! Combat jump in ten seconds."

Sitting back in her acceleration couch she closed her eyes and gritted her teeth as the OpsCen lights dimmed, the anti-gravity cut, and the biocontainment shield fell on her like a dead weight - jumps always seemed to last an eternity.

"Biocontainment shielding up! Stand by for one G in five… four… three… two… one! Lock down over! Weapons free!"

Pulse racing and hyper alert she shook off the dizziness and scanned the dancing holograms - all ship systems in the green, excluding deck seven and the post-jump passive sensor sweep, was clear. So, nothing unexpected or out of the ordinary in *Kumasi's* immediate locality. The almost instantaneous super-light feed from the remote sensors would now have a seven hour twenty-five minutes time lag. Real time info on the Bulges was eight hours away.

"Stand down and set condition SQ2." This signified combat suited but with helmets off - relaxed but alert. *"Naomi, Edzai, I'll take the first watch,"* she announced over the discrete 2IC, 3IC net.

***

"Captain."

Prior to going to sleep one set the command neural net to 'receive' so you could, under certain strict condition, be roused by it. Slowly becoming wakeful, it took her several moments to grasp why she couldn't move freely in her bunk. After all, it had been decades since she'd last hot bunked - one of the few privileges of being a captain or 2IC. Finding herself tightly sandwiched between maleness in a multi-occupant cocoon was not at all an unpleased sensation. In fact, she'd go as far as saying she always enjoyed male intimacy, her issue with the act of sex was being 'penetrated'. Opening her eyes, she slipped out of the bunk without either man stirring and changed into her overalls and ship boots.

That had been Stromme her 3IC who presumably had taken over the watch from De La Haye. A couple of hours into her watch Magambál had changed the alert status to 'routine': it greatly reduced a crew's effectiveness if they were kept at high alert for hours on end with zero happening. Sleepily going to the one privilege reserved specifically for the captain - a mini drinks dispenser in both their cabins - she punched up a coffee then headed for the door. *"Report."*

"Though all appears normal we think we could be under Bulge influence *and may even be under attack."*

Now *that* was an attention getter and well worth waking the captain, though it begged the question of just who this 'we' were. *"Continue."*

"There appears to be two independent anomalous effects. The first was noted in the reinstallation of A/G on deck seven. There was, and still is, a continual three to eight percent fluctuation with the rest of the ship whenever its initialised. After several hours and hundreds of attempts, homeostasis concluded that the most likely explanation is an external gravity influence, they then reported it to the bridge."

Divergent A/G values in different parts of a ship was more dangerous than no A/G at all. Should such an unlikely incident arise, failsafe systems would ensure that it was disabled. *If* the underlying problem on deck seven had been fixed, then the reinstatement of gravity to one G ought to be straight forward. To her mind, the most likely explanation was that the problem wasn't fixed or a new one had arisen. Then again this would also have occurred to Stromme and she certainly would have run that down thoroughly before reporting it to her. *"And the other effect?"*

"The bright neutrinos detectors have begun registering off the scale - the ship is being bombarded with them. To put the flux intensity, which seems to be increasing, into context; it's several orders of magnitude more that we'd use for a super-light jump and we can't tell where they are emanating from."

"Has there been any indication that the enemy ships have changed direction or posture?"

"No, Ma'am."

"*Bring the exec team up to speed and ask them to report in person to my* en-voyage *cabin.*" She was already halfway there.

As far as she knew no intensity of bright neutrinos could be harmful: neutrinos, by definition, were on the subatomic scaled, 'tiny'. If the MMBs could indeed *affect* baryonic matter in our realm by manipulating gravity and bright neutrinos, then it's reasonable to assume that *Kumasi* and her crew were being *affected*. In what way? To what ends? How could they tell? Whatever the answers, the MMBs were expending an enormous amount of energy in doing it. And if they were governed by the same laws of physics then energy had to be the universal cost of achieving anything… That might be a good place to start.

She entered her en-voyage cabin to find all seven of her execs already seated around the conference table-cum-hologram projector. For some of them to have been summoned from the dead of sleep and still be here ahead of her implied that they'd run. On a ship like *Kumasi* that was an artform: they had to move with urgency and purpose but *not* alarm. If the crew saw a senior officer running, something very serious was going down; serious but not panic-worthy. Placing her semi-sealed coffee cup on the table, she took her place and noted the instant wrinkling of noses. Even if she hadn't known it, this would have been a way to ascertain that none of her execs were from Earth. Coffee, or the disdain for it, was an Earth verses the rest thing.

"Does anyone have any ideas or theories on our current predicament?" she asked as she took her place at the table.

There were noncommittal shrugs all round, "Well, let's try and get a handle on how much energy they are expending." She'd addressed the group but was looking at Lieutenant Tori Seckel, her head of engineering.

Seckel had obviously been contemplating this because without a pause she responded, "If we look just at the bright neutrino flux density and make an educated guess of the power needed to enclose a ship the size of *Kumasi* in a gravity field, a very conservative estimate: sixty to seventy days energy output of a sol-type star."

There weren't any verbal gasps or visible signs of shock but 'Motherfuckercocksucker!' 'Holy shit!', 'Well, bugger me 'till I bleed!',' were discernible from the jumbled sentiments that seeped into the command neural net. As neither De La Haye or Stromme was among this collective dissonance, she decided to disregard it. "The Bulges are perennially odd, literally inscrutable, but there has to be a purpose to this. If we are not under attack, then what? And how does it relate to the seven ship we were sent here to monitor? Ideas - no matter how outlandish."

Seckel glanced at Ghanashyam, the new head of homeostasis, before responding. "If we share the same physical laws, then we must share the same space-time. We know it takes enormous energy for them to manipulate baryonic matter in the baryonic realm, so if they begin to expend significantly more, they must be attempting more than mere 'manipulation' in three dimensions."

"Time travel?" Lieutenant Commander Idran Miles, head of weapons, asked dubiously.

Again, Seckel briefly met Ghanashyam's eyes before speaking, indicating to Magambál that Seckel was only the spokesperson, they had put their heads together on this. Good, this is what she expected of her team.

"No, not necessarily," the engineer started hesitantly. "They have the way-with-all to manipulate in the baryonic realm, do they have the way-with-all to 'transfer' from baryonic to the non-baryonic or visa versa. And if they did, what would such a transference look like?"

"Transfer? What, us? That would imply we're being 'taken'. Even if that were possible, how could they keep/sustain baryonic material in the non-baryonic environment?" Lieutenant Seth Leighfield, from navigation, pondered aloud.

"In theory, if they had enough energy, why not?" Stromme, the 3IC, posited.

This was a thought-provoking line of discussion, but did it bear any relationship to reality? She sought a way testing whether they were even in the right ballpark. "Some of you were on the Omega

Zero Three bash and witnessed its destruction, how much energy was needed to accomplish that and how does it compare to that being expended now?"

"Well, Ma'am, if one considers the MMBs manipulations as simply initiating a coalescence of baryonic matter on an atomic level, then Omega Zero Three could be viewed as only a de-coalescence. And I'd guess that that would take considerably more energy that is being expended now - it was a whole planet!" Ghanashyam finally spoke up and took her rightful place among her peers.

"So, if they can generate the energy to toast Omega Zero Three, they can generate the energy to kidnap us?" De La Haye summarised her understanding and Ghanashyam nodded in the affirmative.

"*If* we were being drawn into the non-baryonic, what would we see/experience?" Lieutenant Jacob Friedlaender, from operations, asked of no one in particular.

"That's difficult to say but my best guess is that the changes would be gradual," Seckel suggested hesitantly.

Leighfield leaned slightly forward, "It would be relatively easy to tell if we're being 'relocated': we take fixes on several standard candle stars, Cepheid variables would be best, and note any variations over time."

"How does that help?" Stromme asked the navigator.

"Well, if we were being accelerated at relativistic speeds, we'd note blue or red shifts. If our motion was more modest, we'd see a brightening or dimming, depending on direction. And if we witnessed an all-round dimming then it would be reasonably safe to conclude that we were be drawn into the non-baryonic realm."

"If this were so, we may also possibly detect new non-baryonic phenomena or astronomic objects," Seckel added.

"OK, let's get this mapping started." That was a first decision which Leighfield would be conveying via his neural net. She turned to her weapons officer to issue the second, "Idran, full passive scans for anything out of the ordinary, anything at all." He nodded acknowledgment as she addressed her team, "Any further ideas or suggestions?"

"Standard baryonic weaponry will probably be ineffective in the non-baryonic, but, if it's the same physics then energy weapons ought to still do their job. I'd recommend a contingency plan to route additional power from propulsion to give the lasers more juice," De La Haye suggested.

Magambál nodded agreement then turned to Seckel.

"Assuming we won't be manoeuvring, I can transfer perhaps as much as thirty percent; the weapon systems couldn't handle any more."

Lieutenant Friedlaender shifted uncomfortably in his seat before addressing her, "Ma'am, if they have the power and capability to do 'this', it might be an idea to not provoke them."

"Contingency," she smiled, signalling that she wasn't averse to a little dissention under the right circumstances. Any well-functioning team had at least one cautious component and she was about to discover if she had others.

"Might I also suggest that our first priority on any contact ought to be to understand their intentions, be they hostile or otherwise," Stromme, the 3IC cautioned.

Only a brief eye contact with De La Haye confirmed that they at least were on the same page; *Kumasi* was being abducted and that wasn't a cordial get-to-know state of affairs. Acknowledging that she'd 'heard' Stromme she asked of the group, "Anything else?"

"If we are indeed drawn into the non-baryonic it's imperative that we communicate with C in C fleet. I'd suggest we launch a stand-off drone that we can direct a bright neutrino beam at. It can then relay our messages. The comms will need to be something simple like Morse code." Stromme was much more positive this time. Had she gleaned that she's just underwhelmed her bosses? That would be another good sign: learns quickly and adapts.

Morse code? Magambál has a vague recollection of being compelled to learn the anachronistic convention at the academy, but never having used it couldn't remember any of it.

"I can setup bright neutrino pulses - a beam is too localised, we may be moving in space as well - and we'd probably need several dozen stand-off drones in electronic silence mode to give back-up/redundancy in case they go after them," Friedlaender suggested.

"Speaking of codes, could this bright neutrino bombardment be an attempt at communication?" Lieutenant Leighfield abruptly, and belatedly, asked.

"No. We ran several thousand translator programs for hours looking for any order of Shannon entropy which would indicate intelligent messaging - nothing found," Seckel impatiently brushed off the question.

"OK, let's get on it! Reconvene here in half an hour." Magambál pondered for a second, she wanted to touch base with her 2IC... "Naomi, Edzai stay."

She waited until her other execs had departed before addressing her second and third in command. "This is an 'In all of human history' moment. I want a full, detailed, and transparent briefing of the crew by sections. Impress upon them that though momentous, we should expect everything and nothing, yet be ready for anything."

Before either could respond a rather overexcited Lieutenant Seth Leighfield from navigation gave the equivalent of a shout over the command neural net. *"Nearby stars are uniformly nine percent dimmer than they should be - we must be leaving the baryonic!"*

"Idran, get those drones away soonest! Tori, engines' power on tap to weapons now! Seth, estimate the rate of change! Reconvene in ten!"

She and her most senior officers sat in silence as the remainder of the execs returned in ones and twos. Last to arrive was the new head of homeostasis Lieutenant Ghanashyam who bounced into her seat seemingly bursting with enthusiasm. "Ma'am, I've been thinking that perhaps we might be giving them too much credit. What they're doing may not be all that cleaver. It could be simply that we're not used to thinking in their order of magnitude of energy use." Suddenly realising that all eyes were on her, she took a deep breath and pressed on. "They could be using bright neutrinos and gravity like chopsticks..." Responding to the puzzled frowns around her, she raised a hand and tapped her index finger and thumb together.

"…Pincers. We use bright neutrinos for superlight jumps: to get from point A to B. If we were to liberate our minds of what is possible in terms of energy production, they could be using bright neutrinos and gravity to move us between realms - like pincers!"

Lieutenant Commander Seckel baulked, "The numbers on this would simply be staggering." The engineer had clearly not been consulted on this.

"We unconsciously assume that it's impossible to artificially generate centuries of energy output of a sol-type star, but what if we could not only generate it but also control it precisely?"

"Centuries?" Lieutenant Friedlaender, the ops head tried, and failed, to hide his scepticism.

Magambál thought she'd give Ghanashyam a little encouragement and support while she established her credibility among her colleagues. "Assuming unlimited energy generation; expand on this pincers concept."

"The only fundamental forces and particles common to both realms that we know of are gravity and bright neutrinos. I can't see how either by itself would have any effect *and* we're under the influence of enormous amounts of both."

Ghanashyam now had everyone's full attention. De La Haye leaned towards her. "How long before we're in their realm?"

"Everything the Bulges do is chaotic, but my best guess based on the assumption that the effect started soon after we dropped from superlight, maybe ten to fifteen hours."

"Wait a minute! If they can move between realms, why haven't they done it before?" Friedlaender was still playing the sceptic.

"They are not moving between realms, are they? They're moving us to theirs. To move between realms, they'd have to be able to bring their power source - don't think they can do that, no matter how smart they are." Seckel was back to supporting the engineering/homeostasis collaboration.

"I think we're getting sucked down into the weeds and missing bigger issues." Miles, the weapons head, raised his hand for silence: a potentially insubordinate act when sitting with superior officers. "If we assume, as a working hypnosis, that the MMBs can generate these magnitudes of energy then we're not just talking interstellar, are we? Intergalactic travel would be on the table."

Perhaps it was his expertise in threat assessments that caused him to perceive the potential insects verses highly evolved mammals scenario. Everyone took a moment to absorb this.

"Jacob, flash, tight stream, a SitRep to C n C with our outline theory and plan of action." He was sitting opposite her so she could have spoken to her ops head. In giving him that order over the command neural net she also gave him the authority to convey, to his comms team, that they had permission to break radio silence. She waited until his eye refocused on his surrounding before continuing, "In essence we are a mini battle group. As well as the full ship's compliment, we have on roster one fully equipped marine battalion with their Hoppers and Ground Support Fighters plus one Guardsman detachment so we..."

"There's also a Platinum Stinger aboard, Ma'am," De La Haye politely interrupted her.

"... Indeed, a Stinger, so it's imperative that we think and plan as a functioning battle group and not like a single ship. Options?"

"Well, if we take Cinthia's pincer analogue as a given, then it stands to reason that *if* we were able to disrupt either prong, we'd be freed from their hold and presumably instantly drop back to our realm." Edzai quickly scanned the table for overt dissent, seeing none she concluded, "I'll get a team working on this as our get out of jail card."

"That's an idea. We should have everyone in Suites like we're making a superlight jump," Leighfield, the navigation head suggested.

She nodded her assent to this then said, "Now to prep as a battle group. Edzai and Jacob you've served on carriers: marines, Hoppers and Ground Support Fighters in drop positions. Naomi, I believe you're au fait with Special Ops, once we're tight, ideas on tactical deployment of Guardsman and Stinger. Idran, Tori and Cinthia I'd like options on boosting power to lasers even when manoeuvring *and* do keep those civilians out of the way." She paused calmly look over her team. "To your stations, let's execute, people!"

***

As Ghanashyam had predicted, the transfer to the MMB's realm wasn't constant and as far as they could tell after eight hours they were about 'halfway there.' Everything seemed normal when looking out at the cosmos. Navigation told a different story: in terms of spacetime they were exactly where they were supposed to be, *but* all EM radiation reaching the ship had decreased by forty-seven percent. Now instruments designed to detect baryonic matter and phenomena were starting to act up producing ghost readings.

She was approvingly examining Edzai and Jacob's planned deployment of the ground forces, this image overlaid a representation of the external astronomical state. A ghost image popped-up in the corner of the hologram field, drawing her eyes to it. While this image also faded in and out, it, unlike the other phantoms, had a definite form. It looked like largish spheroid shaped asteroid which sensors located at about a half AU's distance. In the Byronic realm there was nothing nearer than a solitary long-period comet at about seventeen AU's. Having puzzled over it for several seconds she was about to ask, 'What is that?'

"Ma'am, if I may draw your attention to the external representation: the upper right grid," Idran from weapons unflappably came over the neural net. *"It appears motionless relative to our position. We're trying, and failing, to get a lock."*

"It seems to be one of, but not the sole, source of the bright neutrinos." Seth, navigation's head, proved to be equally up to speed.

"Yes... But what is it?"

"Ma'am this..." A replica of the asteroid appeared in the opposite corner of the hologram field. *"...Is, is a scientifically accepted... well-accepted as accurate, simulated representation of a neutron star."* Jacob rather overexcitedly started stammering over the net. *"Its radiation and gravity at a half an AU would be annihilating! That*

thing looks just like we'd expect a neutron star to look but apart from the flood of bright neutrinos there's nothing. Gravity ought to be common to both realms."

A major asset in being an effective captain was 'composure'. "*Say that again but say it slowly.*"

"*Everything we think we know about stellar evolution says that that object is a neutron or quark star composed of missing matter. However, the thing that would confirm it as a neutron or quark star, namely its gravity, is also missing!*"

Magambál pondered this for a moment. "*We've established that the MMBs can manipulate bright neutrinos and gravity in ways beyond our capabilities, couldn't they be masking/minimising gravity's effect?*"

"*But that's a neutron sta...*"

The Head of Operations was cut off by the newly promoted Head of Homeostasis, "*If they have a working theory of quantum gravity which enables them to convert gravity, or gravitational potential, to energy - putting aside the 'how?' - then to all intents and purposes that neutron star is unlimited power... As I've said, we need to redefine 'possible'.*"

On her hologram projection another of the ghost-cum-gravity-deficient neutron stars appeared, it was then immediately joined by a third. Each was approximately the same distance as the first thus placing *Kumasi* roughly in the centre of a triangle.

"*There are two more of these objects, still unable to lock on.*" Idran informed them as if giving simple target reports. She started to consider that his account was unnecessary then reminded herself that not all her execs would be viewing holograms.

"*These are definitely the other sources of the bright neutrinos!*" Seth, her Head of Navigation, announced with satisfaction and finality.

"*So, not chopsticks then but a grapple.*" Edzai, the 3IC, commented deadpan.

Enough of being passive! "*Tori, the ship's structural integrity?*"

"There is no measurable external pressure on the ship, Ma'am," was the engineer's prompt response.

"Although deck seven's gravity won't align, and is still off-line, there is no evidence of extraneous internal forces either, Ma'am," Cinthia added.

"OK. Let's let them know we know they're there and monitor any response." "Naomi, nudge us forwards at ten meters per second."

"Aye aye, Ma'am. Ahead at ten meters per second."

Scrutinising the hologram projection for several minutes she looked for even the merest hit of change to their external situation. As far as she, or any of the ship's instruments, could tell there was none. "Enough of this snail's pace, take it to ten kilometres per second."

"Aye aye, accelerating to a ten kilometres per second."

Another ten minutes or so with nothing from the MMB's: who knows how they measure time? *"Seth, are we still transitioning to their realm?"*

"Yes, Ma'am and the rate hasn't altered in its irregularity."

Magambál switched to the command net. *"Naomi, Edzai, I'm inclined to come to a dead stop and, while still suited and booted, wait until we have something definite to respond to."*

"Agreed, Ma'am. All weapon systems are 'lock and loaded' we can respond at the drop of a hat."

"Agreed. We'll keep working on how to disrupt their hold on us - now we've confirmed there're three sources, this'll be much easier to achieve if we're stationary, Ma'am."

"OK." "All stop!"

Chapter 4

"Really, you are. What more can I say? 'You are literally the best I've ever had'."

"And that soooo goes for me too. Terrific! Fantastic! You're all that a girl could *ever* ask for." Lara-Tilly stepped between him and the gun rack, all girly and flashing eyes.

No lesser official than the ship's First Officer had given them the briefing. He'd also surmised that the marines were getting the same instructions, 'Get prepped and stand by to be deployed into the *unknown*.' Yet, for the first time in countless missions he finally felt he had a sense of the 'tactical situation' and knew some of what the officers knew. Indeed, he would go so far as to say that he actually understood why all the onboard infantry were prepping for this unspecified mission - the captain was configuring her ship to me more like an assault carrier.

With a wanting, wistful stare Rukshana draped an armour-suited arm over his shoulder and in stepping up to do so blocked his other path to the gun rack. "Oh, mover of the Earth, pleasurer of women, surely you are very secure in your manhood?"

"He's so manly that if I could, I'd gladly have his babies." Lara-Tilly affected confidentially whispering to Rukshana.

"Would you really?! Well, actually, I've been contemplating, ruminating, and just doggone speculating about surreptitiously acquiring surrogates for both of us." Rukshana's reply was equally affected.

Lara-Tilly abruptly and dramatically lamented, "Then why oh why does he need a bigger gun?"

It was a simple and single-minded matter: he was never, ever, again going into combat carrying that Guardsman issued feeble, ineffectual, feather duster of a laser. Recon role my arse! When you shoot at something and hit, you want that something to know it's been hit!

"Well, I did erroneously refer to his magnificence as only 'moderately sufficient', Rukshana exaggerated, playing at being beside herself with regret.

"And the old me, the foolishly me had uttered, 'passably adequate'. If only we knew then what we know now." With an equally crestfallen act Lara-Tilly had tears flowing down her cheeks.

Why did it surprise him that they could cry? He's seen Span cry many times and gleaned that a woman crying wasn't necessarily a sign of weakness; it was just one form of venting. It shouldn't have surprised him, but it did…

Something shifted, gravity shifted. It wasn't as if the ship shook or the artificial gravity momentarily malfunctioned, but something about the gravity in their boutique armoury was simply wrong! Rukshana tossed a laser to him and grabbed one for herself. Lara-Tilly was armed, helmet on and at the ready in an instant. While he donned his helmet, his Armour reflexively took up their protective positions either side of him. In the few seconds that he waited for a ship-wide announcement to explain the recent occurrence he experienced a momentary light-headedness.

"We're no longer on *Kumasi*," Rukshana tersely informed him.

Really? He didn't know what was going on in her quantum computing brain, but they were still in the armoury.

"We've experience, are experiencing, something akin to a partial Jump," Lara-Tilly supported her… co-wife's assertion.

No, definitely not. "We're still in the armoury!"

"Not braggin' but most, if not all, of our sensory apparatus is more acute and finetuned than yours. What you're seeing, I think, can best be described as an after-image hologram. I dunno where we are but we are not on the ship!" Rukshana was firm and absolute.

Humour them. "OK, if we're not on the ship why are all the suit's external readout; atmosphere, temperature, pressure, etc., consistent with still being in the armoury?"

Before either could respond he *knew* he wasn't on the ship - he *knew* it as an indisputable fact like he *knew* his name. It was something he'd always known for as far back as he could remember. He also *knew* that the three of them were there because they had earned the Right to Life. *OK this is some weird shit because I know I don't know or understand any of this.* He *knew* that everything about his species and all shadow universe lifeforms, down to the cellular level, was inefficient and wasteful. His 'seemed to have always had' knowledge also contained some perplexity as to why Rukshana and Lara-Tilly had earned the right to life but had not been progeny.

"Are you guys experiencing something like instantaneous implanted memories?"

"Yes," they replied simultaneously.

"Do you think if they are implanting theirs, they could be taking ours and is this a form of communication?"

"Dunno," Rukshana replied scanning left and right. "What are we going to do?"

Of course, they relied on his instincts (rather that his seniority) to determine any course of action. As he contemplated a response Lara-Tilly suddenly raised her laser to the firing position and pointed to a wall.

"Do you see that?!"

All he could see was the wall. He was about to ask, 'See what?' when he noted that Rukshana also had her laser raised and was aiming in the same direction.

"I don't see anything but whatever you do don't shoot. Describe!"

"It's a single crooked three-metre-high tree…" Lara-Tilly began.

"No! It's more like a diseased three-metre-high pinnately compound leaf," Rukshana interrupted.

As he wracked his brain trying to recall what a pinnately compound leaf looked like, his suit finally registered that there was something, four meters distance, in the approximate area of the women's aim. On what exactly that 'something' was the suit was vaguer. Interesting! His Armours' sensory equipment could outdo a recon suit's - this was news to him! Then he *knew* that they had left the shadow universe and were now completely in The Domain of True Existence. He also *remembered* the basic biology of the 'something' his Armour were seeing. He'd always known this, so he accepted it although it was mind-blowing.

Finally, he saw the 'something' and in seeing it instantly remembered what a pinnately compound leaf was. Though it wasn't exactly blurred it was really difficult to define its outline. Dark green all over, the alien - he *knew* it was a singular alien - took on the appearance of a not quite solid three-metre-length branch sprouting what could best be described as seven pairs of opposing mismatching oversized, metre and a half leaves. The creature wasn't just unsightly and ugly it seemed distorted. No apparent eyes, ears, mouthparts, or nostril. Nor any arms, legs, or any appendages for locomotion but it did look remarkably like an enormous fuzzy insect infested compound leaf. But Bataa *knew* that he was looking at *the* top predator.

OK, so why didn't it look like a Bulge? He then *remembered* that the Bulges were just projections into the shadow universe, and they looked the way they did because that was the most efficient form to cull-until-Right-to-Life and then interact with the creatures of the shadow universe.

His eyes were adjusting to this new environment and were 'interpreting' the apparent slight reflections around them as them being in a pool of clear water with lighting above. Yet he didn't feel buoyant like he was in a liquid nor did the suit hint that he was, but that was what his eyes reckoned. "I get the sense that we're submerged, can you detect anything else?

"I don't think we are literally surround by liquid, but... I'm not sure," Rukshana postulated.

"Perhaps we're enclosed in a stasis field or something like that because we are definitely separated from that thing," Lara-Tilly added.

Neither he nor his suit automatics detected any barrier between them and the alien. Because he was actively looking at his HUD, he finally paid attention to the warning light that had forlornly been trying to grab his attention. You always wanted about a third of all resources in reserve in case you ran into the unexpected: the alert that kicked in when the main power level dropped to thirty-three percent was telling him that it was now at twenty-two percent. His Guardsman Recon suit's power ought to last for weeks. Odd! How come both Rukshana and Lara-Tilly had missed that? Even odder! He checked the chronometer: his sense was that they'd entered the armoury about ten, possible fifteen, minutes earlier and the chronometer seemed to agree. "Check suit's power levels and elapsed time!"

"Diagnostics says we're guzzling power maintaining one G, so we must be in a really intense gravitational field," was Lara-Tilly's immediate response.

"Not complaining but why didn't you pick this up?"

"Our suits aren't configured for flesh, so the alert criteria are different and if that thing moves, I'm going to kill it!" Rukshana answered rather aggressively.

Yes, the leaf-thing did look rather fragile, but he *knew* it was anything but. "Don't!" Their Recon suits' instruments would be recording across the full electromagnetic spectrum, but not at a fidelity to match his Armour. "Aren't you both getting a sense that we are… messengers being… primed and we'll be returned to the ship?"

"Yes, we are," Rukshana confirmed.

"Have you been noting and remembering everything?"

"No, but will of now," Lara-Tilly granted.

"Why not?"

"Just like your brain ours also filter out most inputs to avoid sensory overload, OK?" Clearly Lara-Tilly wasn't in the mood for even mild criticism.

"It's gone!" Rukshana suddenly exclaimed.

He needed to accept, and make allowances, for their superior sensory apparatus. Still… "Really? I can still see it."

Both women suddenly started looking around wildly while lowering their rifles. Because he had twisted to tune-in to their strange behaviour it took him a second or two to realise that the alien had indeed vanished, and their mini armoury now had some additional occupants: about a dozen marines. A dozen combat suited marines, all heavily armed, all with their rifles aimed squarely at them.

"*Put down your weapons! Now*!" blared into his headset.

As he very slowly and very deliberately bent to comply while noting both women being equally cautiously obedient…

"*Unsuit then Strip*!"

In the Air Cav a trooper was expected to suit or unsuit in under five minutes, but the twelve or so lasers pointing rock steadily at them, hinted at a much more unhurried approach… This was going to be interesting. How was he going to shield his Armour and their inhuman eyes once they had their helmets off?

"Our mission was classified 'Above Top Secret'. The briefing was given by the First Officer. We will only report or respond to her or the captain." Some of this was the literal truth, some hyperbole, some simply wishful thinking.

That they weren't immediately shot or shouted at hinted at a 'communicating with a higher authority'. 'Safe Mode Activated' popped-up on his HUD... You wouldn't really want somebody wearing a combat suit going rouge on a spaceship. So, any suit could be remotely rendered 'safe' by a senior enough officer. Said rogue individual would still be able to move freely in the suit but was deprived of the ability to tear a body limb from limb.

"*Hands on heads… Left turn… Quick march!*"

Bataa had been part of an escort on a few occasions. These had been ceremonial duties and they always marched *beside* the escorted. All twelve marines remained behind them, no doubt aiming at the backs of their heads with lasers on full power settings.

***

Magambál doubted that any infantry personnel would ever have been in a captain's en-voyage cabin before. Yet standing before her were the four special force infantry on her ship. It had been these four and only these four whom homeostasis had reported abruptly vanishing from the ship's roster. *And* she'd the foresight to have marines at the ready to detain them should they return, re-materialise, re-emerge or whatever.

"Take a seat," the 2IC instructed on suit audio.

Having deemed it prudent to prepare, and bring up to speed, her 3IC on the true nature of the Guardsman Corps she and her two most senior staff sat suited facing the Platinum Stinger and Guardsman. Data from their suits was already downloaded and being assessed by Idran and Tori's teams. Nothing but speculation had so far been reported. All her execs would also be involved in the interrogation via the command neural net, audio only. And every single bit of data as well as this interview was being transmitted, real time, to fleet C in C. Leaning forward she adopted a stern expression copied from Admiral Akobundu-Tan. "Report!"

The Stinger sank into the nearest seat. He then turned to the male Guardsman. "I've partied with a few Guardsman in the past, mind if I take the lead?"

In his suit the Guardsman, Bashe, visibly shrugged assent then also sat. The other two Guardsman followed suit.

"I think I was 'transported' to some half-way state between our realm and the MMB's. I'm sure I wasn't there for long but was subjected to an immense amount of indoctrination. I don't know how they did it, but I feel that I now know everything there is to know about them, it's like I've always known..."

The Guardsman, Thariyan, interrupted. "We were fully in their realm but held in a powerful gravitational field - one much stronger than anything we could generate."

Turning to her, Magambál noted incidentally that the faceplates of the *women's* suits were subtly different; one could not make out the eyes behind them.

"Actually," Bashe held up his hand as if for permission to speak, "I don't think you can begin to understand them or their message if you don't understand their biology."

"Message? OK, what's the top line on their biology?" De La Haye prodded.

"Like us they are animals sitting atop a plant-based food chain, but they go about this in a markedly different way." The Guardsman paused briefly to look at each senior officer in turn before continuing, "Without wishing to insult anyone's intelligence: we eat plants or animal who eat plants by chopping them into little pieces - chewing - then breaking these bits down further before absorbing nutrients in the upper small intestines. With the MMB's they don't chew - they subsume/incorporate the photosynthesising cells of plants, algae or other animals then transport them intact to their skin surface. Here the chemical energy produced by the photosynthesis permeates directly into their circulatory system; all other matter is excreted as waste. Because these photosynthesising cells have only a limited lifespan there is a constant need to replenish them."

"What?!" the 3IC almost leapt out of her seat, "That would mean an ecology consisting exclusively of flora."

"No, Ma'am, just like all known biotics, the animals aren't photoautotrophs and their cells cannot photosynthesise. However, this physiology employs a hyper-efficient form of nourishment. And this hyper-efficiency is a trait that encompasses everything about the Bulge."

Magambál waited for either of her subordinates to comment, as neither did, she pondered aloud, "Hyper-efficient would be the last term I'd think of in characterising the Bulge."

"That's when they're in their realm, Ma'am. And this hyper-efficiency does not only apply to their biology it dominates their lifecycle and psychology. Which is the crux of our difficulty in communicating with each other."

"Really?!" De La Haye made no attempt at hiding her scepticism. "How so?"

Bashe checked right then left to his wives as if seeking support from them, the Platinum Stinger took this hesitation as his cue. "Our progenies have our genes; theirs have their genes and their memories - their essence - so in a sense, they are literally immortal. This is their lifecycle, and it is optimal: they produce many progenies but only a scant few will survive to adulthood and get access to resources. Parents nourish their offspring by supplying them with the photosynthesising cells from their own bodies. When they reach what we'd consider adolescence, just as the progenies are developing the ability to feed for themselves, there is a culling..."

"'Culling' does not accurately convey the enormity of this phase," Guardsman Heye cut across the Stinger clearly eager to redress the limelight being taken from her husband. "It's not only that up to several hundred progenies are whittled down to a handful, it's how this happens. In order to mature the progeny needs to grow rapidly and they do this by absorbing several times their bodyweight in photosynthesising cells. Where do these cells come from? Other adolescents and their siblings! In an enormous gorgefest all the adolescents of a generation set about each other. Cannibalism!"

"Only the survivors of this are considered sentient by the MMB's and only to these do they pass on their memories." The Platinum Stinger seemed persistent in holding centre stage. "They call this stage 'Right to Life' and it is baked into their nature. Right to Life - proving your fittingness, earning the right to become an adult - defines how they view the universe."

De La Haye abruptly sat forward in her seat. "What would you say is the approximate ratio of surviving offspring?"

Bashe hesitantly offered, "I'd say less than one percent, Ma'am."

It took a second or two before Magambál understood where her 2IC was going with this...

"Yes!" the Platinum Stinger proclaimed knowingly, having also 'got it'. "The same usual survival rate after enemy contact. To them science, technology, intelligence, etc. means nothing - only the Right to Life matters. If you haven't been through this winnowing you cannot be considered a sentient lifeform. They weren't attacking us they were trying to identify our adults!"

"I know that sounds farfetched but it's accurate," Bashe corroborated apologetically. "This 'war' was basically them sieving, trying to pinpoint who to talk to..."

"Literally billions have been slaughtered in the last twenty-seven years and you want us to believe they were *basically* filtering?!" She wasn't even remotely ready to buy this... *'Ask why only these four were chosen.'* That was from Idran over the command neural net... "And they decided that the adults were you?"

Even when suited the Guardsman could be seen to shift uncomfortably. "Well, yes and no, Ma'am. From their perspective it's difficult to identify our adults because we don't differentiate adult from adolescent - as they define it. We then compound matters by subjecting some individuals to multiple Right to Life, while most adolescents are never 'tested' - as they define it. What I mean is: although most of the crew must be veterans of many engagements, they don't view the space engagements as combat or a Right to Life situation. That's just them announcing their presence, trying to identify the adults, and gauging our response - which to them is always unfathomable... Although they didn't perceive themselves to be in conflict with us, only planet-side Right to Life counts," Bashe distractedly waved a hand between himself and the Platinum Stinger. "They knew we've had loads of Right to Life."

The Platinum Stinger sat forward exasperated. "Look Ma'am, it doesn't really matter why they chose us, we are in the shit! They didn't think of themselves as being at war with us but know they know we are at war with them."

"Tone!" Edzai, having upped the volume, leaned forwards, and locked eyes with the Platinum Stinger until he backed away.

"Ma'am," Bashe started with emphasised deference, "What we saw as thousands of battles, was them trying to communicate. They interpreted our actions as us trying to respond but instead clumsily disabling their communication devices."

Magambál allowed several moments of silence to pass to let that sink in. "What did they want to communicate with us about?"

"We could explain but that point is now moot, Ma'am. They've in effect given us an ultimatum..."

"What did they want to communicate with us about?!"

"Well this is rather complex..." abashed, the Guardsman started hesitantly.

Thariyan impatiently interjected, "Firstly, because of their near immortality they have a fundamentally different concept of time. Next, they consider their realm to be 'The Domain of True Existence' and our realm as simply its shadow. They have been bleeding energy via bright neutrinos from our realm to theirs in order to reduce entropy there - their objective being to buy them enough time to find a solution to continue True Existence before the universe grows cold and dies. They have been at this awhile: at the big bang both realms made up about six percent of the universe. Now, 'locally' - this galaxy and it's dwarf satellites - it's about seven percent them, five percent us. So, these guys have been operating on galaxywide scale for millions of years. Whenever they encountered a sentient species (as they define sentience) in our realm they offered them the opportunity to 'transfer' to The Domain of True existence. Incidentally, this explains why we find abundant life across space but no signs of civilisations. One possible indication of sentience - as they define it - is the manipulation of bright neutrinos. That potential 'transfer' was what they wanted to talk to us about, Ma'am."

"And that discussion is now moot, because?"

"Well," Thariyan started hesitantly as if lamenting her interposition, "They don't consider us as sentient or intelligent... In fact, I think it would be accurate to say that they currently appraise us as akin to germs that want to initiate a fight."

"Currently?"

Thariyan revealed that it was possible for her too to shift about uncomfortably in a combat suit. "Until we demonstrate that we're at least partially sentient - as they define it - by a culling of the entire human population. If we don't do that, it would imply that we aren't really civilised, then they'll come after us with malicious intent. That's the ultimatum, Ma'am.

"Apparently we're outliers, Ma'am," Bashe diplomatically interceded relieving the pressure on his wife. "It would seem that most of the species they have encountered are similar to them in respects of aggressively regulating their numbers in relation to available resources. And the MMB's deem any 'intelligent' species that does not consciously and deliberately limit their numbers to be a contagion."

"And you got all this from them while you were only absent for..." Naomi checked her one-way hologram, "... less than ten minutes?!"

"I not sure how they did it, but we just seemed to *know* these things, Ma'am."

From the accompanying nods of agreement by the remaining infantry, Magambál accepted that this had been their collective perception. "What else of import that you *know* that we ought to know?"

The Platinum Stinger again leant forward to take centre stage. "Ultimately the MMB's won't allow any species, with the potential to develop technology that could interfere with or reverse their energy outflow, to flourish in the shadow realm. Clearly, we have that potential. Simply put: 'Cull and Join' or 'Don't Cull and Die!'"

When your 2IC and 3IC, both seasoned veterans, starts looking around apprehensively it's time to look like a veteran captain. "Timescales?"

It was several seconds before Bashe hesitantly offered, "Months, years, we're not sure, Ma'am. All I understand is when we're ready to communicate our answer we simply need to return here with a ship that has us four onboard."

"And how, exactly, would they 'kill' us?"

"That we didn't get, but they obviously have the technological prowess to."

"Hang on a sec, there's something I don't get here," the 2IC interjected. "The mighty MMB's are that technological advanced but couldn't tell the difference between a Sap and a human-looking android?"

"They recognise we're human-made and thus perceive us as just another form of inefficient human reproduction," The Guardsman Heye replied angrily.

"Fuck me! You aren't real?" The Stinger exclaimed. "I'd heard rumours but..."

Magambál held up a hand, signalling no more interruptions. "From your intimate interactions with the enemy, any insights on how we defeat them?"

"Surrender runs counter to the entirety of the Stinger creed Ma'am, but there is nothing." For the first time the Singer seemed at a loss. "It's not even to do with technological superiority and their pan-galactic reach. It's their assessment of us as something akin to bacteria. Eliminating the entire human race to them would be mundane and unremarkable as, say, cleaning your teeth." Then he added an afterthought, "It's something they've done on several other occasions."

"Ma'am," Bashe started hesitantly, "I get the sense that it takes them vast amounts of energy to influence events in our realm, like the manifestations of the Bulges. And it took considerably more energy to transfer the four of us to their realm for even that short period..." He seemed to falter mid-sentence.

"Yes, go on," she gently encouraged.

"Well, I think that 'influence energy' cost them transfer time... I mean energy must be the universal currency... They're syphoning energy from our realm to theirs... Every time they try to communicate with us, they must reduce their syphon rate or whatever it is they are doing. If we could make it too costly for them to..." Lost for word he shrugged.

"*We're back in normal spacetime, Ma'am*," Seth announced over the command neural net.

Straightening in her seat she addressed the four. "The fate of the entire human race could be in your hands. Any further suggestion?"

Thariyan pondered for a moment then offered, "Timescale! If we try a wear down and burn out strategy, it would be of millennia duration. We have to find a way to take it to them now and hard."

"Their priority seems to be this energy transfer and from what you're saying, we are simply a minor distraction. So, couldn't we negotiate an agreement not to interfere with the transfer?" The 3IC phrased it as a question posed for general discussion.

Before Magambál had a chance to slap that down the Stinger, Lume, exclaimed, "No! One, you can only negotiate with an entity that views you as a near equal. Two, unless we cull, they won't consider us capable of undertaking any agreement. Three, we'll be acceding to the eventual demise of our realm."

The Guardsman Heye, in a gesture of appeasement to all, shrugged then said, "I think it's fairly certain that *if* the energy cost of fighting us became higher than the energy bleeding to their realm, they would change tact."

Her fellow infantry nodded conveying agreement, so Magambál asked of them collectively, "Did you get any sense of how we may be able to exert influence in their realm?"

"Ma'am," Bashe started hesitantly, deliberately respectful as if forestalling admonition, "I suspect that we might know that. But I don't think we know what we know... I mean, we don't know how to access this knowledge and even if we were able to; would we understand it and be able to communicate it?"

"Well, let's make a start at getting at that knowledge. I want a Contact Report with emphasis on technical information on my desk in two hours. Dismissed!"

Chapter 5

Keeping a crew at high alert for prolonged periods reduced their effectiveness. *Kumasi* was back in normal spacetime, so she'd reduced the alert to a state not requiring the wearing of combat suits... When the hologram of Admiral of the Fleet Akobundu-Tan formed unannounced above her desk Magambál took a second or two to grasp its true significance. The communications time lag ought to be in the order of seven hours or so. C in C wouldn't be receiving any telemetry from *Kumasi* for a couple of hours. Yet here was the Admiral... Let's see: the debrief of the infantry lasted about twenty-five minutes, which ended about an hour and a half ago. So, Akobundu-Tan had been at about two hours superlight comms range, was now 'in the vicinity' and, no doubt, had at least three fleets with her.

"Get each of them one-to-one with a homeostasis technician, walk them through chemistry and physics from baby steps to big boy long pants, see if anything clicks." Without any formality the Admiral cut to the chase.

This confirmed that the Admiral was from Earth. Being fluent in Hungarian was suggestive but this sealed it. Magambál doubted anyone from the colonies would use or understand the 'big boy long pants' reference. She nodded signifying the command as she conveyed it to her subordinates via the command neural net.

"I have some boffins on this, they want the ship's complete sensory readouts, especially those pertaining to bright neutrino flux density."

Again Magambál nodded and set the instruction in motion on the command neural net.

"What's your intuition telling you our next move ought to be, Captain?"

Something about the Admiral's demeanour demanded absolute candour. "We need to get a hold of a way to take the fight to them, Ma'am."

Even with the high-density fidelity of modern holograms she was still surprised to see what she'd consider a predatory approving sparkle in the Admiral's eyes. She annotated that item as number two on her list of things to reflect on when she had a moment or two to herself.

"I concur: our best and brightest are working on the 'how'. Hold position and report any situational changes. The seven enemy ships remain as was. We're standing off eighteen light-years outside the Rancia sector and I expect to be conveying, in the most persuasive of terms, our response' to the MMBs within the next forty-eight hours."

Magambál decided to chance her arm. "'We', Ma'am?"

The Admiral gave a smile that could only be described and deliciously wicked. *"The third, fifth, sixth, ninth, tenth, twelfth, fourteenth, fifteenth and eighteenth fleets."* Then her hologram vanished.

That was everything including the kitchen sink - another idiom that someone from the colonies probably wouldn't get... Unless the MMBs initiated something, they had up to forty-eight hours to prepare for wherever... Mentally she précised the communication with the Admiral then comprised a 'rest and relax but bring everything and everyone up to peak performance potential' instruction before sending it to her exec team. Then with semi-sealed coffee cup in hand she sank back in her seat for some 'me time'...

Was Rancid Roger that good? Could he glean things about her that she barely comprehended? Things that could, in the middle of the most crucial of debriefings, pop up and slap her in the face? It was the Stinger Lume... Even with them both wearing suits, she could perceive the superiority and arrogance oozing from him. Yet something about him brough to mind Sacha. What? Sacha appeared gentle but there was clearly unyielding granite under that boyish surface: he was an assault marine officer after all. Lume also exuded that superficial boyishness but with a hint at a much darker countenance. One is not supposed to become even slightly aroused in a debriefing, but more than once she had to check then tamp down leakage into the neural net because of the egotistical Stinger.

That was on one hand. On the other hand, was Qamar and the deceased Second Lieutenant Sammi Nishioka; her only love. Tough exteriors but soft and lovingly gentle on the inside... The average male (which on the bell curve meant most men) would have approximately equal elements of both toughness and kindness, she supposed. Could this be the reason why she didn't feel the need for relationships with them? Was it just possible that she might only be attracted to the extremes? The dimetric opposites? And dimetric opposites were often very similar: hypoxia and oxygen toxicity have similar symptoms; frostbite was simply one type of burn. Hmm... Another point for consideration was that, statistically, there would only be very few of these men in the general population.

There could be an alternative explanation, of course: in the last twenty-four hours she'd experienced, with Qamar and Sacha, the most carnal moments of her entire life and her *only* amatory exploit in nearly a decade. This could have awoken something... which was now stirring within her. Yes, that was a possibility, but she innately felt it was an unlikely answer - she was only clutching at straws. She had to face up to the stark reality that she might only be captivated by the extreme outliers of heterosexual maleness. Fittingly, that conclusion seemed to slip seamlessly into the arc of her emotional disposition.

Rancid Roger couldn't be that insightful, could he?

What does this all mean?

It means that something within her hankered to be with Sasha and Qamar. Perhaps she should stop viewing it as a distraction and instead now accept it as simply an element of her reality to be persevered like, say, when she yearned for sleep but had the watch... That was easier said than done: she had decades worth of strategies of dealing with lack of sleep. This nascent libidinousness was already portending that it had the potential to become overwhelming.

Then again, any new pleasurable sensation had the potential to be intoxicating and the novelty would probably... There was that subtle beep in her ear signalling that someone sought her attention.

"Captain."

It was Cinthia from homeostasis and Magambál could tell she was struggling to contain her excitement. *"Report."*

"That was a genius idea of yours, Ma'am. Schooling them in basics science is proving to be especially fruitful with the two female Guardsman," Cinthia gushed.

An educated guess was that the Admiral's hunch was being more productive with the female Guardsman because of their artificial brains, which were probably structured around quantum computing architecture. Magambál momentarily pondered whether she should 'read in' all her execs on the true nature of the Guardsman but decided against it, for now. Nor did she want to extinguish the engineer's eagerness but needed it dampened a notch or two. *"Fruitful in what way?"*

"They're both really quite adroit at grasping scientific principles, even complex ones. What is now abundantly clear is that at least some MMB technical knowledge has permeated, albeit at an unconscious level. And we've even been able to inveigle a smattering to come forth consciously, so to speak... Well at least with these two, at any rate." Abruptly Cinthia halted her chattering as if suddenly appreciating that her enthusiasm was hampering her delivery of a comprehensive explanation. *"We've gathered that the MMBs abilities to affect events in our realm is in part because they're using entangled bright neutrinos, which means whatever they initiate here they must be replicating there."*

As far as Magambál was aware humans' science had never achieved entanglement on a practical macroscopic scale. The MMBs were technologically more advanced, so this had merit. Plus, if quantum information cannot be destroyed, entanglement would seem an obvious and logical way to 'communicate' between realms. It would also explain the recent off-the-charts bright neutrinos flux densities. *"How is this 'insight' useful and what use do you propose on making of it?"*

It was, just as Magambál desired, a much calmer head of homeostasis who answered. *"If we were able to collapse the entanglement and force quantum decoherence, we neutralise their effect in our realm, Ma'am."*

Magambál had already thought of this. *"Right, and?"*

"It shouldn't necessarily take us anywhere near the same amount of energy to disrupt as it cost them to construct."

Now *that* was interesting. Her recall of the full gamut of quantum physics theory was hazy at best but something in the dark recesses of her mind suggested that this titbit definitely had legs. *"Have you uncovered any information that, even theoretically, we could reverse engineer so we can project into their realm?"*

"We haven't pursued that angle yet, Ma'am. We get on it now."

Having dialled in, and set, the tenor she expected from her execs in all situations, she was now ready to commend. *"That was really good work, Cinthia. Well done. Pass this on to the remainder of the exec. Report back on any further progress."*

One of the many nuances of the neural net was that it not only conveyed thoughts i.e. information. Often one also got a sense of the feelings underlying those thoughts. She could tell that the engineer was smiling. So was she, but as she began to strategise on the precise tact to take in updating the Admiral on this latest development her smile faded. She had served under several commanders who she, at the time, considered a touch gung-ho so that wasn't the issue. Yet still there was something... something about Admiral that gnawed away at her... Magambál sensed that the Admiral was not only a brilliant and utterly ruthless tactician, she also took delight in confronting danger. Gung-ho on bioadapted steroids - a dangerous tendency in a commander. Then again, she was by far the most successful flag officer...

A second beep in her ear: "*Captain.*" It was Naomi. "*I've been assisting the Platinum Stinger with his Contact Report and science curricula. I believe he has some insights worth exploring.*"

This was the second time her 2IC had emphasise that he was a 'Platinum' Stinger. That she was personally involved in preparing his Contact Report added to the emphasising. Naomi had more experience with ground ops, therefore significantly more exposure to infantry than she had. All she really knew about them was that Stingers were super-special special forces and, as the Admiral had stated, precision instruments. It seemed sensible to be inclined to defer to her 2IC on matters regarding Stingers. "*Go ahead Naomi, report.*"

"*He suspects that the MMBs are... wary of us. In extricating the four of them they ostentatiously display their technological superiority, especially their access to almost unlimited energy sources. Yet, according to the narrative they concocted they've spent the last twenty-seven years trying to establish comms. He strongly believes there's an undercurrent in the information he gathered from them that if they could have simply eradicated us, they would have. Clearly these notions are difficult to articulate and substantiate but he's been insistent and quite convincing.*"

"*You seem to be giving this credence because he's a Platinum Stinger, why?*"

"*To be a Stinger and make it to the Platinum rank and survive there has to be more to you than just being a good soldier. Their historical combat effectiveness and successes defy all logic. They must have a sixth sense, or something and I think we need to consider anything they say even it if is somewhat outlandish, Ma'am.*"

That 'Ma'am' implied that her 2IC assumed she was skating on very thin ice. And she was. Naomi was a *believer*. It seemed to her that the 'metaphysical explanation' had certainly supplanted organised religion as the articles of faith: a belief in the notion that there is some unknown and unknowable deeper connection to the universe that transcends science. This was another of the hotly debated subject on which Magambál remained steadfastly agnostic. Afterall, it'd been only a few months since the revelation of the hitherto unguessed-at realm of the MMBs'. Who is to say that in a month's time medical science wouldn't unearth the underlying reasons why reiki remained the most effective long-term treatment for severe burns. *"OK. If they've been at this for millions of years what, exactly, is it about us that they're wary of?"*

"He's here with me, I'll ask him."

Without warning an emotion surfaced within her, it was so unfamiliar she puzzled over it for a moment or two. At first, she thought it reminded her of times she'd felt professional envy, but this was something else. This was more intense; it was an unaccustomed sentiment - jealousy. Why on Earth should such distracting emotion be surfacing? She knew that Naomi was one of three co-wives of a civilian on Ebury. Bizarre!

"He thinks it's something to do with us being mammals, being able to keep out body temperature warmer than our surroundings..." The 2IC paused, apparently to gather herself. *"Having assisted with his Contact Report, I've concluded that he can't be more precise because what he's recalling is disjointed... Information from the MMBs' manifested itself as memories: knowledge already acquired; facts already known but without anything to anchor them. Progress will be halting because they are navigating seemingly fragments of memories."*

"You've had the summary from Cinthia about the female Guardsman?"

"Yes, that's why I thought I'd bring you up to speed on the Platinum Stinger."

Xenobiology was a mandatory module for any officer cadet of a space services. Though not her favourite subject, Magambál recalled that the mammals of Earth's appeared to be somewhat unusual. Of the myriad animal life so far discovered on other planets, none came close to being like mammals. Most were categorised as reptilian, a few as amphibians, plus several newly defined taxonomic classes, but no mammals. Not even the extra-terrestrial animal species that exhibited thermoregulation to maintain a body temperature higher than their surroundings were mammal-like. At best a few were mesothermic, but most were in some regard ectothermic and could only do so for a limited period.

"OK, if they all have these broken memories, let's have a central repository of their observations. Get a high-level team on cataloguing and cross-referencing. That ought to give us a clearer characterisation of what's really afoot with the MMBs soonest."

"Aye aye. There was something else from the Platinum Stinger: to do with the MMBs using prime numbers."

"What?"

"Now that he's had time to reflect on the encounter, he implores that we not apportion human motives to their actions: that we keep front-of-mind the fact that their mathematics is based, completely illogically, on prime numbers. We must never forget that they are non-static, non-linear creatures who also view us as not having earned our Right to Life. Our very existence is inimical to them and theirs to us."

Understand a cannibalistic species that exterminates ninety-nine percent of its offspring? Hardly. 'Our very existence is inimical to them and theirs to us' - now, that was a mantra worth emphasising to all and sundry. *"That sounds like something he's feeling in his bones and I must confess, I'm feeling it in mine too. Let's make that our refrain."*

***

The collated insights from all four soldiers were slowly sketching out the vague contours of the MMBs: it was our use of bright neutrinos that brought us to their attention. They now had a handle on us and know that we considered ourselves to be in conflict with them - this didn't seem to bother them in the least. Our propensity to reproduce without limits really bothered them: this seemed a contradiction of one of their laws of nature, or something like that. That we'd arisen and evolved so rapidly bothered them: from the grasslands of Africa to walking among the stars in under a quarter of a million years - truly remarkable by their timescales. That our rate of development showed no sign of slackening bothered them. That we'd dispersed so far so fast across the galaxy bothered them. That we appeared to lack 'adult supervision' or collective purpose bothered them. That we would inevitably eventually interfere with their primary goal of extending the lifespan of The Domain of True Existence bothered them. Our energy-hungry mammalian brains really bothered them: this also appeared to contradict another of their laws of nature.

So, if the MMBs had had the capability to take out every single Sap in one fell swoop, approximately seven hours ago, they would have.

They didn't because: to simultaneously locate seventeen plus billion individuals, spread across an area as vast as human-occupied space in a shadow realm, was beyond even their capabilities. And if they couldn't eliminate *the majority* of us in one go then our rapid, geometric progressive rate of reproduction would reassert itself. Consequently, what they 'would like' was for us to reduce our numbers by about ninety-nine percent. Then, and only then, would they grant us the privilege of joining them in The Domain of True Existence.

Should we decline to take them up on their generous offer they will set about reducing our numbers with gusto: by ninety-nine percent would be acceptable. They would then obstruct our use of bright neutrinos thus preventing us from the super-light travel. How would they accomplish that feat? Any artificially generation of bright neutrinos would be instantly detectable in their realm; fractions of a second later they'd turn up and lay waste to that location in the shadow realm. Once we are 'confined to the ground' they can, at their leisure, eradicate our settled planets, moons, asteroids, and orbitals: in much the same fashion as they had Omega Zero Three.

Without endowing them with human-like motives: an unhurried but inexorable extermination, something they could easily accomplish in about three hundred years or so. That was the conclusion of the cross-referencing team, it was also the unanimous interpretation of her execs to the 'gathered insights'. It was what she reported to C in C and Admiral Akobundu-Tan. Having said all that Magambál had, over the many years of captaincy, developed an almost visceral aversion to group think. While she waited for the expected response from the Admiral, she attempted to catechise the entire extrapolation.

First, and most important, the only things we know about them are what they have chosen to 'reveal'. Right to Life: that was simply absurd and truly 'alien'. Their proclaimed purpose: to extend the lifetime of their realm, until they found a cure for the cold death billions of years in the future. If one doesn't have a born, grow old, and die existence but some other life cycle, then that might not be as preposterous as it seemed, especially if they (their memories) lived-on for tens of thousands of years. How could a mathematical system be based on only prime numbers? Defining intelligence or sapience purely on population size vis-á-vis resources, did that seem reasonable? No, ants did that. Hyper-efficiency? She had never seen any evidence of that, just the opposite - a profligate utilisation of energy.

They had taken those four into their realm, ostensibly to communicate. Why those four? Why only four? They have now communicated, of sorts. At least it was intelligible and for the first time we have some idea of their motivations... Well, in fact, we do not. What we have is their 'explanation' of their motivations. Was she being a tad too suspicious? Because, without endowing them with human-like motives, would we bother lying to, say, lice? So many questions but nothing that she could definitively poke holes in. Perhaps she was being overly distrustful, but she would rather be buggered 'till-she-bled than cede her healthy scepticism to anything concerning the MMBs.

The pervasive circumstance of combat personnel, since the dawn of civilisation, was expectant waiting. This was where spending some time with Qamar or Sasha or both might prove beneficial to her mental state. And as she hadn't yet got around to 'both', both would be even better. Keeping her happy and grounded was their purpose, after all...

"Redeploy, my position, coordinates in your NavCom."

No standing on ceremony here: not a hologram just a bleep then the order over the neural net. Magambál could feel it in her bones that whatever the Admiral had in mind it was going to be aggressive.

***

That feeling of professional envy surfaced again as she stepped onboard the Admiral's flagship. *Pantheon* was a fully-fledged Dreadnaught battleship that made her beloved *Kumasi* seem almost whimsical when they pulled alongside. As she entered the Admiral's en-voyage cabin, she was surprise that it was somewhat smaller than her own and, Magambál was pretty sure, smaller than *Pantheon* captain's. When one wielded that much power pretentions were redundant, she supposed. What she wasn't surprise by was to find Rahumaehullah and a couple of other Admirals she didn't recognise also present. There was also the pervasive smell of coffee... Akobundu-Tan was definitely from Earth.

Without ceremony the Admiral waved her to a seat and as soon as she sat, looked her in the eye then stated flatly, "This briefing is A.T.S. Red."

She'd been involved in an Above Top-Secret Red briefing only once before - the euthanasia of the bioadapted. While nodding her acknowledgement she felt both overawed and privileged: she doubted even Commodore Axford would be read in on this... whatever *this* turned out to be.

"Are you familiar with the Fibonacci numbers, Captain?"

Fibonacci numbers rang a distant bell and had she been aboard *Kumasi*, she'd simply call up the info via the neural net. She shook her head.

"Simply put, they pop-up in mathematics and throughout nature and strongly influence our sense of aesthetics. They are linked to what is called the golden ratio: a ratio of approximately one to one point six. This ratio is ubiquitous, well, at least in our realm." The Admiral then held out her left hand as if pointing to her left. "Shoulder to elbow, one; elbow to fingertips, one point six. Wrist to fingertip, one: wrist to elbow, one point six." She tapped her crown with the same hand. "Top of head to navel, one. Navel to soles of feet, one point six. We see it in the shapes of conical shells on Earth, the pseudo-flowers on Panorama, the giant insect webs on Janneri - it is always there, wherever we go."

Magambál got a sense that she was the only one at the table who hadn't known this and now that she was up to speed things could progress. Again, she nodded. The Admiral then shifted her focus to addressing the group. "All available resources have been analysing the data from the *Kumasi's* encounter. And some boffin on Bacci spotted something coming out of the left field that's got Field Martial Nagy and the Joint Chiefs wetting their pants. *Everything* about the MMBs has a ratio of one to one point eight six. And just to move things along: conclusion, same physics but different maths *and literally* a fundamentally different view of the cosmos!"

"I'm not seeing how there can be a different maths. After all, it doesn't matter where you are in the universe, one plus one equals two, Ezocaagbo," Admiral Rahumaehullah was trying, and failing, to sound open-minded.

"I was where you are, Sumudu. So, I had the hypothesis with its all supporting data transferred," the Admiral tapped the side of her head. "Not only does it stack up, it answers an awful lot of questions."

On one hand Magambál felt favoured as if she'd been enrolled into a very exclusive club: Admirals wouldn't normally use each other's first names with subordinates around. On the other hand, downloading information direct from the neural net into one's brain was of course straightforward, but such acts carried high risk of neurotrauma such as a stroke and/or encephalitis - everybody knew that. The very least you'd walk away with, if you could still walk, was a severe long-lasting headache. Akobundu-Tan didn't strike her as reckless or desperate; there had to be more to it. That the other Admirals didn't seem too surprised or bothered hinted at some above-her-pay-grade technology which mitigated the harmful side-effects of a net dump.

"We already suspected that their numbering system is based on prime numbers but couldn't began to fathom the whys and the wherefores. What's becoming evident is that everything we do, including the mathematics we invent, is based on our *interpretation* of the world around us and I don't just mean us using base ten because we have ten fingers. We use maths to put order to what we *see*. We *see* the golden ratio in even the shapes of spiral galaxies. So, what do they see when they look at those same galaxies? Whatever it is, it's something completely different to us. Top line: they aren't only in another realm they are in another *understanding* of reality!"

"And why are the Joint Chiefs excited about this?" the woman to Magambál's right asked in the slow drawl of someone from Rancia.

"It explains why nothing they do makes a lick of sense. It explains the time it takes them to range-in on us. It explains why they think it's possible to prevent the cold death of the universe. It explains that we don't need to understand them, we just need to disrupt them. And it explains how to achieve that by dragging them into an energy deficit. Would you like to know how we're going to take it to them, Sanaz?"

Putting the face to the name, Magambál realised she was sitting next to the illustrious Admiral of the Fleet Sanaz Araki, commander of the tenth fleet. She had a reputation for being so bloodthirsty that some thought her capacitor couldn't hold a full charge. The word on the street was she'd spat out her dummy and thrown her toys out of the pram when she wasn't invited to the Omega Zero Three play-away-day.

"Oh, do tell."

"You've all seen the reports, they have tamed neutron stars - that's their power source. To take a neutron star and make it of practicable use, they are supressing/containing its immense gravity. Whatever the mechanism of confinement, physics dictates that it must be quantum mechanical in nature - probabilistic and inherently unstable.

The energy around the table changed as if a rapacious eagerness had suddenly manifested itself. Not for the first time it occurred to her that an innate bloodthirstiness might be a prerequisite to becoming a Flag Officer.

"They can blanket a solar system wide area in bright neutrinos for days if necessary. They are also clearly able to affect gravity, on a local level. The boffins are confident that *if* while thus engaged they get hit with an enormously intense beam of bright neutrinos, from any direction, at any angle, emanating from any realm; it *would* take the shine off their day."

"How would we generate, focus and then target such a beam? They are neutrinos after all," Admiral Araki asked thoughtfully, her mind obviously already scheming.

"A missing matter neutron star suddenly undressing, being caught au naturel so to speak, in their realm would also have a damn big impact in our realm too, wouldn't it?" the other Admiral asked before Akobundu-Tan could answer.

Turning to him Akobundu-Tan gave a sly smile. "Agreed, Tom. Would have to be a shoot and scoot."

Tom...? To Magambál's knowledge there wasn't an Admiral Tom Anybody. Pondering for a moment she recalled that there was, however, a flag officer who carried the moniker *The Tomahawk* - Admiral of the Fleet Majid Bin Sharin. Nicknames were rife throughout the military but to have one accompany you all the way up the ranks to Admiral was unusual to say the least. For instance, the last time anyone dared call her by her nickname 'Clip', was the day she was promoted to a First Officer. Whatever it was he'd done to earn that nickname must have been epically audacious or foolhardy... Shoot and scoot? She suddenly felt it in the pit of her stomach: that was why she was here, and she immediately started fretting for *Kumasi*.

"Stop teasing us Ezocaagbo, let's see your plan," Admiral Rahumaehullah leaned forwards, all smiles and eager.

A hologram of a cruiser with a thermo-ceramic outer shell, but thankfully not *Kumasi,* appeared above the desk. "As Sanaz's stated, focusing the beam of bright neutrinos is the technical challenge. This is the mid cruiser *Mies*. It suffered major damaged at the Merrs Twelve jamboree and is currently on its way here at maximum speed from the Bacci shipyards with a skeleton crew. According to the boffins, if a ship this size or larger were to *discharge* its superlight drives in a prescribed manor, without actually jumping to the superlight, an energetic directional pulse is the result..."

"And the ship's destroyed," Sharin muttered.

"... not a beam but damn near." Akobundu-Tan then looked her in the eye despite Magambál being sure she hadn't released an audible sigh of relief. "There's only one ship with four particular individuals onboard that the MMB's want to talk to..."

"It will need to be microseconds between *Mies* dropping from the superlight and *Kumasi* having to jump," Rahumaehullah mused.

"Easily enough done, we synchronise their atomic clocks and set a countdown," Araki offered.

"OK, let's say we pull this off, our long-team strategic goals are?" Akobundu-Tan retook control of the conversation then answered her own question. "We put, and then keep, them in an energy deficit. Taking out just one of their neutron stars ought to dissipate/redistribute a significant amount of energy back in our realm. And now that we know what to look for, we go hunting their power sources."

"Not by sacrificing ships but developing specific weapons to kill missing matter neutron stars," Sharin nodded to himself.

"Field Martial Nagy assures me that's already in hand," Akobundu-Tan confirmed.

"Their likely response is to retaliate but that would drain even more energy. Even so, what's our defence strategy?" Araki asked pensively.

"Yes, that would work," Sharin said in agreement to something.

"No, identify a respectable number of their neutron stars and hit them simultaneously, they need to know we mean business," Rahumaehullah asserted somewhat forcefully.

"Let's stop ascribing human rational and motivations to them, shall we?" Akobundu-Tan said to no one in particular.

The communication between the Admirals momentarily took Magambál back to being at the Academy surrounded by her intoxicated fellow cadets when she was completely sober. Then it dawned on her that not only were the Admirals receiving information, she was not privy to, from a neural net; the commanders of the other fleets were obviously also involved in this discussion. This might explain why she sensed that they were comfortable in each other's company but there was also a tangible hint of underlying professional rivalry.

"*Mies'* ETA nine hours so let's use the time to pinpoint targets within striking range!" Araki was so forceful Magambál thought she was going to bang her fist on the table.

"The *Mies Kumasi* dance is the testing of a hypothesis at the cost of one ship. Once it's proven the manufacture of bright neutrino pulse weapons becomes priority number one and then the Joint Chiefs will have us partying like it's going out of style." Though still convivial, Akobundu-Tan's tone had changed from the conversational to the instructional. "We'll use the nine hours to prepare for their response whether we're successful or not."

***

He hadn't especially warmed to the Stinger; however, they had been briefed by the captain herself. Although located in the same armoury, they were ordered to not carry, touch, or think about weapons of any sort. It transpired that at the last transition into the MMBs' realm the Stinger had been in a Jump Suite. There was a brief discussion about repositioning him here but in the end, it was decided he should be positioned in his original Suite. After less than ten minutes in their respective locations it became clear that this fellow, Lume, didn't respect matrimonial boundaries. Nor did he seem to find anything off-colour in unsubtly propositioning, over the open net, in turn Rukshana then Lara-Tilly. Why? They were physically separated, suited and were likely to remain so until mission end. He certainly wasn't from Earth and polyandry was the norm in the colonies. Behaving as he was, he had to be from somewhere polygamous like Ebury or Janneri.

It was also obvious that although he knew they were androids, he hadn't adjusted to the fact that he wasn't dealing with 'typical' women. This didn't necessarily contradict the explanation he was given by The Armourer; Stingers and Guardsman went their separate ways thousands of missions ago. The chat between them was fascinating and quite amusing to listen to. No one had thought to endow his wives with a 'how to deal with unwanted advances' subroutine. They were, after all, Guardsman who would supposedly only ever interact with other Guardsman. But the persistent bugger kept his blatant advances on the right side of one of them wanting to go find him and stuff their fists down his throat. But if the situation did indeed escalate to an actual coming to blows, Bataa figured the Guardsman combat suit would win, it had significantly more armour that a Stinger's.

After a while he separated himself emotionally from the escalating missteps and miscommunication at inveigling. Leaving it to run its course, he refocussed on the task at hand. In this mission it had been impressed upon them that they carried the hopes of the entire human race for peaceful coexistence with the MMBs. Deep down he felt this was an admission of defeat but accepted that it was obvious that they faced a vastly superior enemy. Even so, we Saps have so much more fight left in us... He arrested the thought: another point emphasised for this mission was them consciously thinking and projecting *feelings* of peace and reconciliation. Taking a deep, calming breath, he reiterated to himself that there was no disgrace in defeat if you'd fought valiantly. Still it hurt... That's it! The Singer was keeping his thoughts off warfare...

The armoury suddenly began to shake violently, and they bounced around like pebbles in a maraca: even the suits' automatics and stabilising gyros were swamped. After about a minute the wobbling haphazardly started lessening and he *knew* he was entering The Domain of True Existence. By the time the shaking had subsided to the point they could stand, it seemed as if they were still in the armoury but now it was filled with a liquid. If that were so, why was there no sense of buoyancy? Checking his HUD, he expected to see a similar power expenditure maintaining one G as last time. What he saw instead was an external gravity reading of one point seven G; nothing his suit couldn't handle. But power was being depleted by the suit automatics maintaining integrity against a near catastrophic external pressure of six hundred and eighty-seven atmosphere.

He *knew* that they had been brought to this shallow depth because their inefficient, feeble shadow realm physiology and primitive technology couldn't survive any deeper. Then the surroundings of the armoury gave way to them hovering mid-air surrounded by what appeared to be thick, dark brown swirling clouds. There was no fading from one environment to the other, just an abrupt change. Despite finding himself suspended in churning wispy vapor, with visibility only a few metres, he didn't experience disorientation or vertigo It took him a moment or two to realise why: the absence of any feeling of being suspended, his vestibular system knew which way was up. Something blinking on the HUD drew his attention: the outside temperature was minus a hundred and twenty-six degrees C and the suit's automatics were trying to resolve the contradiction between temperature and pressure. They were also hesitant on defining whether the external atmosphere was liquid or gas.

Then he *knew* that the demonstration of a full shift to The Domain of True Existence was successful. Obviously, Saps couldn't survive in this environment but a suitable one would be found once they had completed the Right to Life. His eyes were telling him that there were shadows moving about in the swirls, but he *remembered* that at this depth movement was sluggish. Along with this memory came an *understanding* that the MMBs were aquatic but in this place, in their natural habitat, they swam in a medium that was both liquid and gas or more accurately, could be either.

"All my sensors are functioning, but can't make sense of what's out there," Rukshana stated rather hesitantly.

His suit also confirmed that all detectors were operational, but there was serious vagueness about what exactly was being detected. Interesting! They had been briefed that their - of the baryonic realm - sensing equipment would not work if they were taken fully into the MMBs' realm. Disorientation including but not limited to dizziness was highly likely. So, working sensors meant what...?

"That means our suits, and probably us, are now composed of missing matter. And I can't see any of you, nor are you registering on my HUD," Lume announced flatly.

Both Lara-Tilly and Rukshana were right there in front of him but neither of them nor Lume registered on his HUD. Looking around he couldn't see the Stinger. That in itself didn't mean much, the visibility was at best ten metres and his Jump Suite must have been at least... Did he just suggest that we're made of missing matter? Before Bataa's brain had time to reject that notion out of hand, another element from the briefing asserted itself: MMB technology might seem like magic but keep front of mind it's just that, technology, which given enough time we would develop. Though he felt it a bit of a stretch, *if* he was now, by some near miracle, made of missing matter why did he feel exactly the same? This was insane! If every atom in his body had been replaced with missing matter atoms, was he still himself? What exactly, was it that made him, him?

"All our suits are time synchronised. I'm pinging Lume's and getting no return which should indicate significant distance but there doesn't appear to be any radio comms delay," Rukshana informed them.

"Also, we're supposedly floating in a liquid/gas, but the footing is firm beneath us," Lara-Tilly started hesitantly. *"Additionally, have*

you noticed that the pressure is lessening, which would suggest we're ascending. Lume, does this comport with your situation?"

"Affirm, but the light doesn't seem to be coming from above. In fact, there doesn't appear to be a source or prevailing direction," Lume confirmed.

Taking a pace to his right confirmed Lara-Tilly's footing observation and the HUD now indicated an external pressure of six hundred and three atmosphere. Keeping an eye on the pressure readout showed that yes it was dropping. But it wasn't doing so in a consistent fashion; the changes were so haphazard that he was surprised he wasn't feeling any motion. As for the light, he had hadn't been aware until Lume pointed it out: it was the same brightness in all directions and, even more unnerving, he couldn't see any shadows cast by him or the women. He still didn't have a clue as to the whereabouts of the Stinger. "Nothing hostile so far so let's just roll with the blows and see what they have in mind. Remember to think pleasant conciliatory thoughts." That last sentence even sounded hollow to him.

"Look! Three O'clock." Lara-Tilly didn't quite manage to keep the alarm out of her voice.

One of the shapes was much nearer and had resolved itself into something slowly moving around them that looked... simply wrong. Try as he might, he couldn't think of a single thing that the form reminded him off. Bataa realised that his mouth was gaping open while he observed this thing that was literally beyond description. Then he realised his Armour had sprung to their protective positions on either side of him.

"I'm also seeing something, but I can't define or describe it," the Stinger sounding awestruck. *"What do you see and a second or third opinion would be not go amiss."*

Bataa suspected that Lume wasn't accustomed to asking for help and that was as near a plea as they were going to get... The Stinger had seen something peculiar approximately the same time they did. How could they have seen the same thing but not be able to ping each other? He was about to acknowledge equal ignorance when he *understood* that Lume was someplace else and the object they'd all seen posed no danger. Hang on a sec, Lume wasn't here but was seeing something that was here? Or was the thing, whatever it was, both here and there...?!

"As the captain said, we're bound to see and experience many unusual phenomena. Let's try and tamp down alarm and stay emotionally warm and cuddly, shall we."

Was Rukshana having a dig at the Stinger...? He was *baffled* that he didn't know when the Right to Life would be completed... Then *frustrated* that he didn't know if it had started.

"Shit is gonna get serious!" Lume needlessly cautioned.

Chapter 6

She had been briefed and had briefed her exec team. And as with all good tactical plans it was simple: *Kumasi* having synchronised its atomic clock with *Mies* was to return to the exact spot where he had transferred to the MMB realm. As soon as they began to experience the effects of intense gravity and bright neutrinos, they'd flash the first signal. By this time Akobundu-Tan would have dispersed the combined fleets all over the Rancia sector broken down into baby flotillas. The expectation was that the MMBs would initiate communication with the four infantrymen and because they could read minds the soldiers were charged with conveying that they would like to open a dialogue prior to starting negotiations.

The instant one of those non-baryonic neutron or quark stars was positively identified, the second signal would be flashed along with the star's comparative position in the baryonic realm. Then the clock would start running: twenty-seven minutes and thirty seconds later *Kumasi* would auto-jump. A fraction of second later a crewless, fully automated *Mies* would drop from the superlight and detonate. In the twenty-seven minutes and thirty seconds interval, all detected non-baryonic neuron star's position would to be plotted and transmitted.

Homeostasis had reported the infantrymen's absences several minutes before a positive ident on the non-baryonic neutron stars but, as with the last encounter, there were only three of the behemoths. The second flash message had been sent twenty-five minutes ago. Everything and everyone was set, there would be only a ten second countdown. Then an auto-jump of only three point five lightyears: far enough away to be out of the 'blast zone' but near enough to jump back into any ensuing fight if necessary. Whether we managed to destroy their neutron star or not, the likelihood was fight there was going to be: predicated on the assumption that the MMBs would lose their minds and come after them with malevolent intent. Every missile silo, railgun port, and laser battery was armed, manned, and ready; this was going to be a hot jump.

She made a final visual check - all greens except deck seven's bothersome failing artificial gravity. *Kumasi* was already throbbing as his superlight engines spooled-up. "Weapons free, Number One."

"Aye aye. Weapons free, Ma'am."

'Weapons free. Pre-jump. Weapons free. Pre-jump.'

The artificial gravity cut simultaneous with the lights changing to red and dimming then the biocontainment shield dropped on her, as it always did, like a lead weight falling.

'Lock down! Lock down! Combat jump in ten seconds...'

Having steeled herself to the inevitable unpleasantness of the jump, she knew something was wrong from the outset. Her sense was that the jump, which should have lasted seconds, was dragging on for what seemed several hours. Something was very wrong. Though her eyes were shut tight, after a while she started seeing blinding pulsating lights which triggered a pounding headache. She'd never had a migraine, but this incessant throbbing tallied with what sufferers described except amped-up orders of magnitude. Something was very wrong. Whatever the timespan of the jump it had been long enough for her to have soiled herself several time. Fortunately, combat suits were designed to accommodate that as well as take care of its occupant's basic needs. Something was very wrong. At some ill-defined moment she realised that her fists were clenched so tightly her fingernails were stabbing into her palms though the sheer-proof fibres of the gloves and drawing blood. Yet she couldn't summon the wherewithal to unclench her fists. Something was very wrong. Agonising cramp crept up and slowly began to assail her entire body because it was being held rigidly in one fixed position for too long.

Something was very wrong. As a child she'd seen a hologram of a killer whale shaking a seal pup to death and despite being enclosed in a biocontainment shield she suspected she knew exactly how that seal pup felt. Something was very wrong. Her jaws were clamped so tightly for so long they began to hurt, and she was sure she'd cracked a tooth or two. The intensification of the perceived stresses on her were so high she was physically incapable of relaxing. Something was very wrong. Her entire being felt wrung-out as if subjected to severe, months-long physical abuse. This wasn't just the usual strangeness caused by a jump. The sensations of *this* jump were unique, discrete, never before experienced. She also knew she was going to puke, something she hadn't done in years. Something was very wrong.

'Biocontainment shielding up! Stand by for one G in five... four... three... two... one! Lock down over!'

She tried to view the hologram status readouts dancing like distant stars above her. Her eyes refused to focus and even if they had, tears streaming profusely blurred her vision anyway. She just managed to clumsily get her combat helmet off before vomiting. She desperately wanted to hear status reports on *Kumasi* but all she heard were the multiple moans, groans, and spewing of OpsCen personnel being sick. She needed to focus on the wellbeing of her crew and ship but all she could manage was to lie on the couch taking deep breaths simply trying to return to a semblance of her normal self. After a while, a determined attempt to simply raise herself off the couch ended in abject failure as if she and her stomatic nervous system had undergone a ghastly divorce. Striving to call up hologrammatic schematics that would indicate the health of her ship failed because she could not manipulate the controls due to the trembling of her hand.

Minutes were passing and her ship might be in danger, but she couldn't muster the energy or enthusiasm to even sit up. "Report," a feeble croak was her best effort.

There was what seemed an interminable amount of time before she heard, *"We're lost,"* that pronouncement was form Seth

Leighfield who sounded like he was giving birth. "*Star density, types, and ages suggests we must be near the centre of the galaxy. Trying to get a fix from the local group galaxies.*"

Even in her befuddled brain-state she knew a position fix from external galaxies would be, at best, imprecise. A positional fix required known-spectra stars within the Milky Way... Near the centre of the galaxy...? That would mean they'd travelled tens of thousands of lightyears: had she been in a peppier vein, her estimation would have been more exact.

"*Jump time thirty-nine hours, twenty-one minutes... Ship-wide life support systems set and stable... Artificial gravity still disabled on deck seven.*" Cinthia from homeostasis said between soft sobs but her voice also sounded different, like she'd developed a lisp.

Even at maximum superlight speed they couldn't have travelled thousands of lightyears in forty-hour jump time. She attempted to guesstimate how far a forty-hour jump would be. Ahh my head hurts... The air circulation system in the OpsCen was losing the battle with the stench of vomit, so what must it be like in a Jump Suite?

"*All weapon systems online, manned and ready.*" Idran was, as always, calm but also sounded in pain. "*External radiation levels suggest that we're only a few light years outside the ring of dust and gas orbiting Sagittarius A-Star,*" he added, agreeing with Seth's assessment of approximate position.

It was impossible... she revised that thought... Travelling thousands of lightyears in a forty-hour jump went against all the known laws of science! And that persistent pounding headache declined to ease off.

"*All systems operating within parameters,*" Tori whispered feebly, as if this took the last of the engineer's vigour to make that brief report.

"*Full passive and active sweeps completed, no external threats.*" Naomi's voice was barely audible.

She was being a terrible captain, she tried sitting up, swayed, and flopped back into the couch - this must be what it feels like to be drunk or drugged... "Set alert state to routine; maximum passive scan; bring all automatics online; crew to rest and recuperate. Execs, what happened?"

The silence was so lasting she was tempted to ask the question again...

"*Captain,*" Jacob from operations meekly and apologetically reported, "*Medial jump teams are logging an untypical number of crew reporting post-jump emotional disturbances. Additionally, many more are reporting skeletal damage caused by severe muscular spasms. There is also a preponderance of reports of crew biting off bits of their tongues. Most of the casualties are in Jump Suites, overwhelming the ship wide medical jump teams. Infantry and spaceborne combat medical teams are taking up the slack.*"

"Numbers?"

"*Approximately thirty-eight percent of the crew are registering for medical assist.*" That was delivered so feebly it was obvious that was all the 'talk' Jacob had in him for now.

"*I've triple checked: we are near enough to Sagittarius A-Star to detect its gravity. I have also crossed checked our jump time and can confirm it to be thirty-nine hours, twenty-one minutes.* Seth tossed the time/distance paradox on the table in case it had slipped past anyone. In not furnishing an answer to her question he'd simply doubled down on the need for one.

"*As expected, the sensor logs recorded a seismic spacetime event immediately after we jumped but the energy readings are literally off the scales - spiking beyond our instruments registry. That's significantly more than we'd expect from unshielding a neutron star, even if all its energy were transferred to our realm.*" Idran paused as if waiting for someone to comment when no one did he continued, "*We're talking a Type II supernova energy release here and, in terms of the fabric of spacetime, like an elastic snapping.*"

"*So, you're suggesting that somehow we were catapulted here?*" Edzai, sounding more perky than most, spoke for the first time.

"*Well, it's a working hypothesis,*" he did not sound particularly confident.

"*We have an approximate fix; plus or minus four parsecs; on your screens,*" Seth announced for the navigation team.

Scowling she looked up: that was no fix at all. Four parsecs was over twelve lightyears. Space was *nearly* empty, but it wasn't *completely* empty. For superlight navigation purposes one wanted an accuracy of zero point one astronomical or less. It didn't matter whether sub or superlight, flying into anything more substantial that interstellar gas was pretty much the end of the line... The projection sprang into life, but it still took her a while to bring it into focus. The graphic revealed the Rancia sector and human occupied space to be on the opposite side of the Sagittarius A-Star supermassive black hole and the densely populated galactic center. It explained why the fix was so coarse, only a few of the known-spectra stars were visible from here...

"*There is no way we could have transit across that!*" Cinthia managed to convey assertiveness with indignation tagging along while simultaneously seeming physically spent. "*The only way to get here, in the time we did, would be us travelling 'through' a rip in spacetime.*"

That assertion made Magambál's head hurt even more as she tried wrap her brain around it.

"*I know it's a challenge explaining our current position, but we need to stick to the 'possible'. Anything in the proximity of a Type II supernova would be obliterated! If spacetime somehow got ripped, we would have been torn asunder with it.*" The 3IC wasn't prepared to give this any credence.

"*Wormholes have been hypothesized for centuries and a supernova is just the kind of event that could generate one...*" Jacob began to suggest.

"*A wormhole that conveniently just happened to be at our locale and of a size where* Kumasi *could fit?*" The 2IC's threw her hat in the ring in the 3IC's corner.

This was descending into an ill-disciplined squabble which she was about to slap down, hard. Then she checked herself; if she was feeling fragile, short-tempered, sore, and exceedingly anxious so were they... Humour. "We bombarded, with bright neutrinos, what we guessed would be a neutron star confined in what we guessed would be some type of unguessed-at quantum field. Now we're guessing at how, exactly, we got to be here. Let's keep everything on the table, even the impossible. We are dealing with more advanced technology, after all."

"*Ma'am, I've took the liberty of reading-in the chief engineer, Vinson Belmonte Muñoz, who is a superlight propulsion specialist,*" Tori started in a sort of timid, dipping her toe in the water manner. A wise move because there was using one's initiative, then there was breaking the chain of command. "*He has some insights he'd like to share.*"

"OK, let's have it on the table, Vinson." She hoped she conveyed a relaxed attitude because she wasn't sure how formal to be with a civilian who was only supposed to be along for *Kumasi's* shakedown. As for Tori, the jury was still out.

"*Well, hello everyone,*" he begun as if addressing a symposium. "*The energy spectra couldn't be from a Type II or any kind of known supernova: the x-ray and gamma ray proportions were simply wrong. But they are consistent with a category of neutron star. I mean of course a magnetar, all-be-it one that would have to be rotating hundreds of thousand times per seconds.*"

"*Is that rate of rotation even possible? There has to be a limit to spin angular velocity,*" Naomi's tone emphasised that the 2IC was simply questioning, not challenging.

"*The gamma and x-rays relationships point to a magnetar. The energy output dictates very rapid rotation. Also, being cocooned in a magnetar's immense magnetic flux density might explain why we're still intact - the ships shielding is patently inadequate at protecting against that order of energy discharge.*"

"*But we'd jumped to superlight... But, then again, if the spacetime was being distorted...*" Seth started the sentence before developing his reasoning.

Vinson's participation brought an informality that was just what was needed to reduce tension. But Tori still wasn't in the clear. "If were to run with the magnetar and magnetic flux density idea, how does that move us forward?"

"This might be shedding light on a puzzle that I'd put on the back burner. The physical description of an actual MMB suggest that they are aquatic. And the question that's been nagging at me is, how does an aquatic species begin to harness and then build electronic technology?" Jacob appeared to assume that the solution to his conjecture was obvious.

"And?"

"Well, electricity is obviously the basis of all our technology. Them being aquatic could mean that their technological base is magnetism."

"And given enough time, harnessing a magnetar would logically be the pinnacle of their technological achievement. That could offer possibly even more energy than a fusion reaction." Vinson took to the notion enthusiastically.

Something about all this also resonated with Magambál but how would magnetic technology work in practice...? In the end it didn't matter. Nor did it really matter how they got to be here. Post-jump shock was no excuse, as the captain she'd asked the wrong question. What happened wasn't the issue. "OK, we need to rest and recuperate. The priority is to re-join the fleet in the most timely and efficient manner. Let's reconvene my en-voyage cabin in six hours with a strategy. Mr Belmonte Muñoz, you are welcome to join us." And Tori was off the hook.

"I'll take the first watch, Ma'am."

Magambál was genuinely surprised to find Naomi standing next to her couch. She knew she was a couple of years older than her 2IC so not a single cell in her body was going to argue. She started to swing her feet off the reclined couch...

"Seven enemy ships have materialised: two five five: thirty thousand kilometres. Closing!" Idran was again Mr. Calm.

"Action stations!"

Naomi spun and started sprinting back to her OpsCen post and as Magambál reached for her combat suit's helmet she felt a twinge of sympathy for those who had puked inside theirs.

'*Action stations! Action stations!*' boomed over the tannoy.

Her crew were far too fragile to fight. "Stand by for emergency jump! Nav, set an evasive course, then program jump."

"*We're inside a globular cluster, the matter density is too high to make a respectable jump. We haven't had time to determine enough fixes.*"

We don't even know where we are, so how did they find us? How is it even possible to track and locate a solitary ship across thousands of lightyears? Can't run, can't hide... She'd seen reports of a newish tactic that hindered the MMBs planetside when in their Bulge form: time to see if it worked in space when in their ship form. By her reckoning about twenty-five minutes had passed since they'd dropped from hyperspace "OK Seth, here is the sequence I want: program in a suitable jump even if it's a few AUs, we remain at that local for five minutes then auto-jump back, to a dead stop, midway between where we are now and where they materialised. Keep that jump sequence encoded; to be executed but in reverse. Jump when ready!"

"*Aye aye, Ma'am: jump, five-minute wait, jump to a dead stop current midpoint, then ready for reverse. Jump soonest.*"

"*All weapons still online, locking on targets. In range in two hundred and eight seconds,*" Idran confirmed.

Three minutes and twenty-eight seconds until we're in range of their weapons, they'd have to be much closer for ours to be effective... This is where her navigation team earned their money: make the slightest error in their calculations and we die; take longer than one hundred and ninety-seven seconds and we die. Nail-biting waiting would simply exacerbate the strain on her already over-stressed crew. They needed to be occupied. "Ops, homeostasis, I want everything locked down now!"

'*Stand by for no-notice combat jump! Stand by for no-notice combat jump!*'

"Engineering, as soon as we drop from the second jump, I want max power diverted to the lasers, even if we overload them. Naomi, Edzai augment Idran and his team with targeting. The instant they are in range, I want seven first shots, first kills."

"*Depending on their precise relative bearing if we rotate longitudinally, we'll bring most or all rail guns and lasers into play,*" Edzai offered.

"Good idea. Idran, how many seconds to discharge all tubes and empty guns?"

"*Including reorienting the ship, I'd say approximately eighty to eighty-five seconds.*"

"OK, that's the plan." Even at close range it ought to take the erratic MMBs longer that ninety seconds to acquire them.

'*Lock down! Lock down! Combat jump in ten seconds.*'

She hadn't been counting but her internal clock said 'only seconds to spare' as the biocontainment shield dropped. It was only a short jump but her already distressed constitution started to react dreadfully, yet she was determined to fight through it and stay mentally razor-sharp - *Kumasi* and her crew demanded it of her... The instant they dropped to normal spacetime she puked-up in her helmet, evacuating what must have been the remaining contents of her digestive system.

'*Biocontainment shielding up! Stand by for one G in five... four... three... two... one! Lock down over!*'

A few minutes of strained post-jump silenced passed before the reports commenced...

"*We've jumped twelve AUs and are still completely inside the cluster.*"

"*Full passive and active sweeps completed, no external threats.*"

"*Ship-wide life support systems set and stable; artificial gravity still disabled on deck seven.*"

"*All systems operating within parameters,*"

"Enemy Ships?"

"*If they are still around, they'd be just outside detection range.*"

Now was not the time to be squeamish; unfastening her helmet, she tipped its contents on the floor, shook it once firmly then determinedly clamped it back on. Her crew desperately need the five minutes of respite. "OK, patch me through to all stations." She took a deep slow breath through her mouth. "This is the captain. Sitrep: as I'm sure you all realise; we've jumped a considerable distance. By unknown means we've been catapulted to the other side of the galactic centre. Seven enemy ships have traced us. We've broken contact and will jump to reengage in a few minutes. After we discharge all munitions, we will break contact by jumping again. And we will keep at this hit and run until all enemy ships are destroyed. Sit tight, focus, perform as I know you can, we will prevail!"

A brief glance at her 2IC and a faint nod of approval from Naomi was all the communication needed. "OpsCen, after we drop if they aren't in-situ, it will be only minutes before they appear, stay sharp!"

'Weapons free. Pre-jump. Weapons free. Pre-jump.'

'Lock down! Lock down! Combat jump in ten seconds.'

***

The surrounding environment abruptly changed. There was no sensation of motion or any visual clues but 'here' was someplace different to 'there'. They were still submerged in a liquid, still at many atmospheres pressure but they were unquestionably somewhere else. His suit was trying to tell him that the external environment consisted of something that may be nitrogen dioxide, but it couldn't really make up its mind. What it was more confident about was that 'this' atmosphere wasn't identical to 'that' atmosphere. He *knew* a significant event had taken place: not good not bad just significant. This was the underlying impetus for their relocation. Sizeable amounts of energy had been lost and was still escaping back into the shadow realm. In terms of the human pledge to Right to Life he *remembered* 'yes', 'no', 'maybe'...

"Think about it! Individually and collectively yes, no, maybe - one word. or two words, or three words." Lume was attempting to sound blasé but failed to keep the excitement out of his voice.

Wherever 'here' was Lume was still nowhere to be seen but in radio range.

"What?" Rukshana demanded, not disguising any of her annoyance at his gibberish.

"They only use prime numbers so to them an idea or knowledge or information can only be true, false or unknown. They are trying to grasp the concept of lying; 'yes, but it's really a no' and applying it to our intentions re: a truce and Right to Life."

They don't get lying. Why would they think we were lying? Because no matter what we have been told, deep down none of them accepted or truly believed we were going to just roll over and give in to the MMBs - it went against human nature. Bataa felt this in his bones. So, this would strongly suggest that MMBs could delve even into their unconsciousness. Or something had happened to prompt them to question our sincerity and the answers might be in their unconsciousness. How does one, even an alien, not understand lying?

He *understood* that another Sap miscommunication was the cause of the energy loss and considerable resources were being devoted to staunching this. For some unknown reason the visualisation of a bucket leaking popped into his head. OK, but for a bucket to leak there needs to be a gravitational potential: what gradient that would cause energy to want to leak back into the shadow realm? Bataa guessed that if such a gradient existed then the MMBs must have built the equivalent of a dam. Then he *knew* the MMBs were using his and the reactions of the others to access whether it was miscommunication or a deliberate hostile act. The scales were falling on the side of hostile act, but they couldn't figure out why.

How do you not understand lying? "Do you sense that you've changed location and what's your assessment of the state of play?" he asked of Lume.

"Yes, I've moved. I think a party has started but we weren't invited..."

"*Or we were the invitation,*" Lara-Tilly interjected.

"*...but I don't see how we could dance to cause them any duress, but they're definitely upset about something.*"

Just as he started to worry, he *remembered* that the three of them and Lume had already gained Right to Life and keeping them alive necessitated getting them back to their ship in the shadow realm before their suits' life support gave out. And, in the current circumstances, that was proving problematic. In general dealing with the virus like Saps was proving problematic.

"OK, so something has kicked off, it involves us, Saps, doing something that could be interpreted as either miscommunication or hostile. They're inclined to think hostile but can't figure out why we'd want to be hostile when we said that we wanted to be friends..."

"*'We' were told the Saps wanted to be friends,*" Lume corrected. "*Putting aside their dilemma; a more pressing matter. Do you get the sense that they can't hurt us, I don't mean don't want to, I mean 'cannot'?*"

"Well perhaps..." He *remembered* that he had a Right to Life. "Holy Shit! It's literal! Kill any that don't make it, those that do, *must* live! Is that what you're getting at?"

"*Yeah. That's why they can't eliminate the Saps: some have a Right to Life, and they can't distinguish who.*"

"*It not necessarily that they can't differentiate, they have identified us, haven't they? So, a logical explanation is that the process of discrimination is energy-costly,*" Lara-Tilly suggested.

His wives might not have a theory of mind, but they were clever. "Yeah, but let's see how they managed to do that? Let's say they engaged a battle group on some planetary assault or other. Ostensibly this is simply to identify the Sap adults. After that engagement they'd be, what, thirty or forty thousand..."

"*On a good day.*" Despite him not being visible one could tell Lume had shrugged.

"...OK, let's say twenty thousand survivors and about a third would have been planetside. How do you identify and keep track of seven thousand individuals from another realm? That must be energy-expensive."

"No, they can't identify and keep track because if they could, they wouldn't have a problem," Lume sounded certain. *"If the could; after they'd finished with us only a teeny, tiny minority of the human race would be alive."*

"They can obviously identify, tracking for them must be the issue. That also dovetails with their wayward targeting," Rukshana stuck to her guns.

"And if they only deal with prime numbers, four doesn't compute, which explains why you aren't here." Lara-Tilly added.

"OK, so what should we do?"

"Maybe ask them to place us on land, it's the pressure that depleting the suits' power."

He'd asked the question of Lume but it was Rukshana who answered. Then he *remembered* that they were on a gas/liquid world and at shallower depths there would be creatures large enough to crush their suits. In the totality of human explorations of space to date, not a single animal has been discovered, that was powerful enough to even scratch a combat suit. So, it wasn't only the MMBs that were dangerous.

"I don't see any option but to wait while being alert to changes in our circumstances," Lume offered positively.

Bataa *remembered* that returning the three and the one to their ship was still problematic and their suites' power reserves were running dangerously low. Then the realisation hit with the force of a right hook: any species that eliminated ninety-nine percent of its offspring to prove fittingness took living seriously, very seriously indeed. The insight he had was that the Saps naturally zeroed in on the ninety-nine percent eradicated and, as a mortal species, couldn't even begin to get their brains around how the one percent would view their place in the universe.

***

'Biocontainment shielding up! Stand by for one G in five... four... three... two... one! Lock down over!'

"Full passive and active sweeps completed, no... Contact! Seven enemy ships: three, two, four: fifteen thousand, three hundred and eighty kilometres."

"In range; multiple lock-on!"

"Fire!"

Lights dimmed and *Kumasi* reverberated to a rhythm of the pop-whoosh, pop-whoosh from the missile salvos overlaid with the chest-throbbing infrasound from the scores of railguns' linear accelerators. On screen were the images of the seven, neon blue, always changing shape, super-sized enemy vessels - even *Pantheon* would appear tiny next to one... The bi-frequency laser hits registered first: their efficacy being confirmed by the shadow puppet ships spontaneously fragmenting into wiggling rope-like kilometres-long columns then the majority, but not all, of the still wiggling columns instantly recombining to form a slightly smaller ship: inoperative columns slowly drifted apart lifeless and still. The less observable depleted uranium impacts joined the lasers: the fragmentation rate took a noticeable fillip. Then the showstoppers with their firetails and eye-wateringly bright detonations arrived. The intensity of the fire was such that each enemy ship was fragmenting and reforming so rapidly that they looked like a mere outline of a ship, surrounded by a haze of debris which was gradually, almost ethereally, increasing in volume.

That's what seven first shots, first kills look like...

"All silos discharged; guns empty."

"Switch power back to engines... Jump!"

'Lock down! Lock down! Combat jump in ten seconds.'

During this very brief superlight jump she felt in a very literal sense that all she wanted to do was to curl up into a ball and cease to be.

'Biocontainment shielding up! Stand by for one G in five... four... three... two... one! Lock down over!'

She had heard of dry retching but hadn't believed it was an actual thing. Now she knew better but wasn't going to complain, she was enclosed in a combat helmet after all. The sensation of wishing to quit living, to find sweet release was almost irresistible. There was only so much that the human nervous systems could take. She was certain that if they were forced to jumped again her crew would become not only nonfunctional but suicidal.

"Reload...! Damage report."

"Full passive and active sweeps completed, no external threats."

"No damage reported."

Kumasi's clean bill of health came as a relief. MMBs weaponry tended to detonate inside ships as if teleported in and even a single hit could inflict serious devastation. "Damage assessment."

"All pre-jump readouts confirm all ships destroyed. We killed them." There was no jubilation in Idran's tone just exhaustion and relief. *"Rail guns reload completed; silos twenty-seven percent stacked, complete in eight minutes. Sixty-eight percent of munitions expended."*

Using her physical self as a template she made a rough calculation. "Seth, I want a course back home within three hours. Ready to jump in four; ship wide sanitising, rest, and recuperate until then.

"Ma'am," Ghanashyam from homeostasis surprisingly made contact over the command neural net rather than intra-ship comms. *"My team has reported that every time we jump to superlight, traces of the four infantry biosignatures register. It is as if they were, by some means, still connected to the ship."*

Hmm... That could be how they're managing to track us. Her crew were incapable of engaging in another fight. "Belay rest and recuperate. Sit tight until ready to jump." Sit tight mandated remaining in or being in close proximity - thirty seconds close - to a Jump Suite. "On detection of any enemy ships auto jump to a dead stop our original position."

'Sit tight! Sit tight!'

"Auto jump programmed."

Yes, this matter needed to be restricted to the command neural net. *"Cinthia, clarify these trace biosignatures."*

"Having analysed the readouts; all four register momentarily, for less than three seconds, as being fully in situ just before and immediately after each jump. Then their signatures instantly vanish."

"Could they be in some way still anchored to the ship, thus enabling the MMBs to locate us?"

"That thought had crossed my mind Ma'am, but I couldn't begin to posit on how they achieve that. We really don't have a working hypothesis about how they are able to transfer them to their realm."

"Are you sure that they register as being fully 'here' both pre and post jump and not as shadows?" Jacob from operations gently probed.

"Yes, as if you could touch them. Why do you ask?"

"I think this timing is significant. If there was some connection, then post jump would make sense; a reacquiring so to speak. Pre jump is insane. How could they possibly know we are about to jump?"

"Easy: they see the supersaturation build-up of bright neutrinos which, incidentally, takes about three seconds. When we drop from superlight, they see the discharge of surplus energy," Tori explained then added. *"That, however, would imply we are under continuous surveillance."*

Such an eventuality would be disturbing. *"Idran, precisely how long after our drop did their ships appear?"*

"Twenty-eight minutes and thirty-one seconds, Ma'am."

"Seth, are we holding a static position relative to the surrounding globular cluster?"

"Affirmative."

If they knew where we were all along, it means it took them twenty-eight minutes to emerge their ships at our locale in our realm. Only twenty-eight minutes when it took us thirty-nine hours, by whatever the means that was, to get here. *"I think it's reasonable to assume that in about twenty-eight minutes, or so, more of their ships will materialise. Edzai and Jacob, all ground support ops and ops resources to assist navigation with the plots. Seth, time is a luxury we don't have; I want us on the move sub-light in fifteen minutes; ready for first jump in twenty. Concurrently plot subsequent jumps..."* She did a quick whole-of-body health check and some rough calculations. *"...of five minutes duration, followed by fifteen minutes rest and recuperation. Cinthia, make whatever adjustments you see fit to reduce the stresses on the crew. Everybody else stay sharp, they might not give us twenty minutes."*

As Magambál listened to the readback confirmation of her orders some flashing anomaly on her hologram display caught her eye. She stared in disbelief for a moment or two; it was an icon of one of those MMBs' phantom neutron star...

"We're under bright neutrino bombardment again and this time the flux intensity is orders of magnitude higher. We're being pulled into the non-baryonic realm!"

Cinthia failed in her attempt to sound composed and she'd definitely developed a lisp, probably from biting off a piece of her tongue. "Auto jump, now!"

'Lock down! Lock down! Emergency jump in ten seconds.'

It would be a very shorty jump and she hoped that only a small proportion of the ships compliment, especially non-operational like the infantry, would have had time to wander more than ten seconds from their Jump Suite. Even so, she was sure that, after the pounding their central nervous systems had taken, it was inevitable that there would be casualties. Afterall, her inners felt like they had been bitch-slapped. When she opened her eyes to try and focus on the anomaly's plot position, using her physical state as a template, she knew there would be post jump fatalities.

'Biocontainment shielding up! Stand by for one G in five... four... three... two... one! Lock down over! Sit tight remains in force. Jump medical teams to all Sectors and all decks.'

"Belay jump medical teams deployment." She couldn't see the anomaly on her screen but that could have been a result of her blurry vision. "Bright neutrino readings?"

'Jump medical teams stand fast.'

"*Normal, and we're back in our spacetime...*"

Idran cut short Cinthia. "*That thing is still out there at maximum detection range and I think it's moving towards us.*"

"*Captain, with assist from ground support ops, automatics, and ops, navigation can plot five minutes jumps and providing we get about forty-five minutes to replot and rest we can take incremental baby hops home.*"

Seth sounded more desperate that confident but given the situation she'd take desperate. "*Can we take that first baby step now?*"

He took a while to answer which, in the specific instance was acceptable to her: he was checking with someone and then double checking. "*We'll have the plot and be able to jump in three minutes.*"

"*Idran, do we have three minutes?*"

"*I think so, it's moving in our direction but not directly.*"

"*OK, Seth plot and auto jump in three minutes!*"

"*The jump medical teams to deploy and assist; window two and a half minutes.*" Naomi, as 2IC, was rightfully rectifying the omission thus taking some of the pressure off her captain.

'*Jump medical teams to all Sectors and all decks. Window one hundred and fifty seconds.*'

"OK, patch me through to all stations... We have, in a single action, confronted and destroyed the seven enemy ships stalking us. To my knowledge, in the twenty-seven years of fighting the Bulges, no crew or ship has ever taken on and taken out more than three enemy ships in any one engagement. And even in those circumstances the vessels accompanied an enormous battle group. Well done everyone! In three minutes, we will be making the first of several short jumps. Our aim is to plot and move; jump toward home before they can detect or zero-in on us. Seven confirmed kills to *Kumasi* and should they attempt another attack we will take it to them once again. Sit tight and be ready to jump!" She hadn't intended to project being so belligerent and bloodthirsty but now that she had, she felt invigorated.

Captain ... Ray Anthony

***

"What was that?!" Lara-Tilly asked in alarm.

Before he could even begin to think about an answer he started being bounced around and shaken violently. All that he could really discern with any clarity was the ceiling, floor, walls, and the occasional gun rack in the armoury as he ricocheted off... Well, sort of. Although every rebounding felt like it was unequivocally and definitively off a solid surface, visually things were more ambiguous. At times, his surrounds appeared to be him still submerged in the high-pressure gas/liquid. This was not as it was when they were taken into the MMB's realm but in reverse. No, this was considerably more chaotic in its harshness.

'Biocontainment shielding up! Stand by for one G in five... four... three... two... one! Lock down over! Sit tight remains in force. Jump medical teams to all Sectors and all decks. Set condition SQ2. Jump in T minus forty-five minutes.'

Eventually, and it did seem as if it lasted an eternity, he bounced off a wall, flew across the width of the armoury, smashed into the opposite wall, then landed face up splattered on the floor. No doubt, if he hadn't been wearing an extremely snug-fitting combat suit, he'd have suffered serious injury or possibly death. Moments later Lara-Tilly squatted over him and unceremoniously flipped him over and began tinkering at his back of his suit.

"You know the drill, you can't hold your breath for as long as we can: power with air, and water dump."

When his still spinning eyes in his still stupefied head finally focused, the suit's biometric readouts were a steady red, and the power indicators were flashing alarmingly - the ringing in his ears had swamped the audible alarms. He'd assumed it was the vigorous shaking and the brutal impacts that were the causes of his acute tinnitus and hallucinogenic dizziness. As the suit's warnings became less glaring and more hushed his feelings of euphoric soaring swooning diminished. He took a deep breath, slowly sat up and looked around to double check that he was where he thought he was.

"Where's Rukshana?

"I'd guess about three quarters of the distance to Lume by now. I shouldn't worry, she'll get here in time. And now husband, you can unsuit at your leisure or stay suited and simply power-up at your leisure." She connected her suit to the ship's power supply, took off her combat helmet, ran a hand through her untypically long hair then winked at him.

"I think the ship just dropped from superlight."

"It did." She was staring intently into his faceplate. "Are you OK? You looked off your face." Without waiting for an answer, she began to remove his helmet.

It wasn't until he'd pulled in a lungful of crisp, Earth subtropical, circulated, ship's air that he recognised that he was still a little lightheaded... Enough of this mollycoddling: he made as if to move her hands away but with their heads being so close together she took that as his intent to kiss her, so she kissed him. It wasn't just a peck on the cheek kiss either, this was more your serious carnal activity is about to ensue kiss. Where was she going with this? They were both wearing combat suits! In answer, she daintily sprang to her feet and impatiently started unsuiting. She had no theory of mind but surely she wasn't thinking about...

"Get your suit off and get naked!"

The brain compartment that wanted to take some time to assess just how seriously to take this 'instruction' was instantly overridden by the compartment that *knew* she was dead serious...

"Report to the Captain's en-voyage cabin immediately," blared out of a concealed tannoy. It sounded like the First Officer.

'Safe mode activated,' their suits simultaneously informed them.

Chapter 7

The first, and most noticeable, thing of note was how fresh-faced and full of the joys of spring they looked. It wasn't until these four soldiers returned that it became glaringly obvious that everyone onboard *Kumasi* appeared absolutely mashed: looking, sounding, and moving with all the grace of the living dead. Dressed in their respective black and sky-blue one-piece suits plus the Guardsman donning sunglasses, the infantrymen should have seemed ludicrous, begging to be the butts of ship wide jokes. Yet compared to the rest of her ship's complement they simply looked the part!

"Report!"

"Top line, Ma'am," the Guardsman stated quickly as if determined to have his say before the Stinger. "They've got our number and... I don't know how I know this, but I do... they are going to wait us out..."

"Think of them as literally Gods - in the Greek sense." Not to be outdone the Stinger sat forward cutting across the Guardsman. "But because of our Right to Lives they can't eradicate all of us. Their plan is to wait beyond the lifespan of those who have earned a Right to Life then they'll come after us with malicious intent."

The female Guardsman, Thariyan, held up her hand in permission to speak. "They are not barbarians, there is an alternative. Likewise, I don't know how I know this, I just do: in my memory are the technical details of what we'd call generation ships - spaceship designed for sub-light interstellar travel. If we eschew bright neutrinos technology, they'll leave us alone. If we don't, they will end us!"

"People, I think we're getting ahead of ourselves!" the 2IC forcefully interjected. "What the hell are you talking about? We took out one of their neutron stars and *Kumasi* just buttfucked them in a seven v. one.

Thariyan reacted as if the been slapped in the face but the other female Guardsman sprang to her aid. "Is that what happened? It would have been a magnetar and to them that was like the malfunctioning of one fuel cell, in one cluster, on one ship, in the fleet." Realising that she'd probably overstepped the mark Heye checked herself then modified her tone. "The ships you attacked weren't hostile they were the mean by which the MMBs were attempting to return us after they had moved *Kumasi* to safety. And in trying to understand them..."

"*They* moved the ship to safety?"

"Yes, because there are other Right to Life onboard."

The Stinger leapt to his feet. "Look, I wasn't joking about thinking of them as literally Gods! Their abilities and view of the universe are so far beyond us..."

"Park your arse!" The 3IC was now also out of her seat squaring up to the intemperate Stinger.

"Ma'am," Bashe began, attitude and tone deliberately calm and respectful. "I think information is revealing itself to us that we only realise we know when we say it... To the MMBs Right to Life is everything and they, well, their memories, live for epochs. So, to try and gain any understanding of them and their motives it might be expedient to consider them Godlike."

The Stinger abruptly sat back down and Edzai followed suit while Bashe was speaking, but Magambál could sense Naomi primed, ready to shoot this down, so she pre-empted her. "Let's say for the sake of argument they are divine, expand on this moving *Kumasi* to safety and those ships not being hostile."

"It's really about the fact that in trying to communicate with us they created our Right to Lives. Once they had created us, they were obliged to ensure we live. Whatever happened to the magnetar would have destroyed the ship, so they moved it out of harm's way..."

"We're on the other side of the galaxy!"

Bashe took a slow, deep breath then started back with an apologetic 'don't shoot the messenger' expression. "I don't think we can relate, in the true sense of the word, to their perception of distance or time or any other metric, Ma'am."

"OK, go on."

"What you perceived as seven hostile ships were three portals for us, plus one portal for Lume, and one plus two portals in reserve - they were determined to keep us alive. When you destroyed them, they had to use more 'unrefined' means to get us back aboard. Returning to our realm was a much rougher transition that going."

Magambál began to feel an ache in the pit of her stomach. The engagement and multi-jumps had resulted in a hundred and thirty-eight fatalities and serious physical and mental injuries numbering in the thousands: possibly all for nought. "Sub-light interstellar travel?"

"The MMBs are prohibiting us from super-light travel. The have given us the technological knowledge of cryogenics suitable for a warm bloodied species like ours and the specs for sub-light generation ships. This will retard our spread in the galaxy, but more importantly give us time to evolve. You see, everything about a homeothermic species is an anathema to them. Biologically we require a surplus of energy plus all our technology produces waste, usually in the form of heat. Their biology and technology are geared to utilising every joule of generated/captured energy."

"And if we defy them, they'll come after us?"

"No. Because we lied to them, they have given up on us as a species. Their verdict and response is already in place: the clock is already running, so to speak. *If* after a predetermined lapse of time, comfortably longer than a human lifetime, they detect our use of bright neutrinos they already have mechanisms in place to eradicate us. We don't know what these are, and I don't think we'll be able to find out."

"*They could be lying*," Idran offered over the net.

"How can we be certain that this is so?" Edzai demanded.

The Stinger turned to face her, exaggeratedly respectfully so. "Well, firstly, in their realm a happening or idea is either true, false, or unknown... Intentionally false doesn't really exist there. And even if they were inclined to, we aren't significant enough to lie to." A beat passed before he added, "Ma'am.

"It's not just that," Bashe quickly interjected heading off the borderline insubordination. "They know we have no biological means of extending our lives or preserving our memories and, to them, artificial methods won't count."

Nonsense! She couldn't believe that she'd begun to give this any credence; chastising herself for that, she inquired, "Really? What about your Armor? They are, by definition, 'artificial methods' are they not?"

"Ma'am, we cannot outlive our Guardsman and any attempt to alter that would negate what makes us sentient beings and our Right to Life." Thariyan was also overtly attempting to de-escalate the friction permeating the en-voyage cabin. "The MMBs have given us one lifetime to stop superlight travel, stop superlight communications, stop utilizing bright..."

"If he dies, you die?! That must be a real pisser!" The Stinger exclaimed. "How do you..."

"Button it!" Edzai snapped at him.

It took her a second to clue in to the underlying sexual tension percolating between them. She was fairly sure her 3IC wasn't consciously aware of this and equally sure the Stinger was and intentionally provoking her. She opted to not react emotionally and silenced him with a stern look then focussed on the male Guardsman. "So, they are going to quit until this predetermined lapse of time?"

"Yes, Ma'am. No matter what, I don't think there will be any comms with them again, ever."

"Seth, start plotting to get us home expeditiously. Cinthia, get everything and everyone shipshape ready to jump in T minus one hour."

"On it!"

"Aye aye, Ma'am!"

Returning her steady gaze to the Stinger she asked, "As a Platinum Stinger, what is your recommendation on out best course of action?"

Clearly taken aback he fidgeted in his seat for a second or two before answering. "I know that all we've said must seem dubious and fanciful, but I wasn't being hyperbolic when I said we need to think about them as Gods: there is an unbridgeable chasm between us and the MMBs. Our twenty-seven-year war has been only fleeting, to them. Straining the limits of our technological abilities to engage them was no more than an annoying distraction, to them. My recommendation would be to adjust our civilisation to sub-light travel while ensuring we do not regard it as a regression."

She shifted focus. "And your recommendation Guardsman Bashe?"

"Ditto, Ma'am. But I'd add: no secret projects, no attempts at circumvention, no trick! Now that we've lied to them, they have us under continuous scrutiny."

"Surely if that were true, they would have to expend enormous amounts of energy pulling something like that off in our realm." Naomi was clearly not buying it.

"Yes, but insignificant compared to the energy disruption a homeothermic species could cause... And I think our actions have confirmed that assessment."

"Guardsman Heye, Thariyan do you have anything to add?"

"In terms of freeze, flight, fight I have *fight* installed into my base programming. So, when I say I concur that we need to abide by their diktats I do not say so lightly." Thariyan answered solemnly and Heye nodded in agreement.

"They are not Gods! They are not invincible! We took out one of their power sources; we can take out more!" Naomi wasn't going to relent.

"No, you won't be able to, Ma'am. The magnetars are only detectable when partially immersed in our realm," Heye replied respectfully.

She checked to her left then right to see if her 2IC or 3IC had further questions; neither did. "Thank you. Grab a bite to eat, we will be jumping within the hour. Dismissed."

***

Her crew still couldn't endure long jumps, so she eventually retired to her en-voyage cabin during the sixth forty-minute rest and recuperation stop. The moment she sat behind her desk she regretted it; now she had time to think. Although she'd taken casualties before, she'd never lost a ship. Any action against the MMBs, (née Bulges), *always* resulted in high attrition and high casualties: that was baked in and taken as a given. So, one hundred and thirty-eight dead should be considered light... Thariyan had said that female Guardsman were programmed for fight. Reluctantly Magambál conceded that she too had been programmed for fight. She was only twelve years old when her parents finally relented and enrolled her at the Naval Academy. Perhaps their reluctance had been well founded. Freeze? Flight? Fight? The enemy mega-ships were *known* to be only a means of communication. It was *known* that what we'd interpreted as aggression was them attempting to ascertain our 'adults'. The seven 'enemy' ships hadn't initiated any hostile acts, nor had they made any threatening moves. Now a hundred and thirty-eight of her crew had died in a non-battle.

At lease they'd managed to circumnavigate Sagittarius A-Star at the galaxy centre and established long-range comms with the fleet. Though communication at that range was sketchy, the news was more positive: after *Mies* exploded there was an instant quasi-Type II supernova but there were no reports of enemy activity in, or near, the vicinity. When *Kumasi* didn't show-up at the RV point at the expected time plus half an hour, it was assumed he'd been lost. Having transmitted the full recording of both the seven-ship contact report and the infantry debrief they got, because of the distance, only a receipt message from the Admiral that all had been taken under advisement...

The hologram projector bleeped, signalling a comms request from Qamar.

"Yes."

His hologram formed showing him to be calling from MedCen. She immediately lamented sounding so officious, but he smiled his roguish smile; instantly lifting her spirits. "*Magambál, a thought: it'll be over half an hour before we jump again. Why don't you take a break from the bridge? Sacha is in the cabin.*"

For the first time, in a long time, she was feeling unsure and vulnerable and at a loss on how to communicate it... "Magambál is what mum and dad call me, call me Clip."

"*Clip? A play on 'magazine' by any chance?*" He blew her a kiss and, most surprisingly, she blushed.

"Perceptive." She blew a kiss back. "I take it you won't be joining us?"

"*No, there's literally thousands of jump-induced injuries being attended to. You go take the weight off.*" This time a wink accompanied his smile.

Staring at the fading hologram she pondered a term for how she was feeling just then... 'Being thought about...?' No, not quite... 'Being cared for.' The captain of a heavy cruiser needing tender loving care? It pained her to concede that Rancid Rodger might be on to something...

This time the beep sounded in her head simultaneously with the appearance of Admiral of the Fleet Akobundu-Tan's hologram. For hologrammatic comms to be already working she figured that the fleet must be moving at high speed to intercept *Kumasi*... A second hologram took shape a few second later: Field Martial Nagy, boss of the Joint Chiefs.

Uh-oh!

"*Captain.*" The Field Martial nodded a perfunctory greeting. "*Please summon the Platinum Stinger and Guardsman.*"

She did so, also reading-in her 2IC and 3IC, via the neural net then gave both Flag Officers her best deferential but insistent 'I want an explanation' stare. "They are on their way, Sir."

"*Their debrief has reached the highest levels, so our response will now be a political matter,*" Akobundu-Tan explained. "*And as you would expect, there is a great deal of scepticism.*"

"*Specifically, around issues on just how seriously to take this 'threat',*" Nagy added after a while.

For Nagy to be involved in this conversation, albeit with a greater comms-lag, meant that he couldn't be on Earth. The Old Bugger must have come out to play. The boss of the Joint Chiefs freelancing? So, the *Mies* vs neutron star gambit had probably been viewed as the pivotal point of moving from defence to offence... What a bloodthirsty lot.

"*As the one who conducted the debrief, what's your take?*" Akobundu-Tan pensively asked.

"Well, all four certainly believe what they were saying. The cryogenic and generation ships' specification has definitely been placed in the quantum computing brains of the female Guardsman - it's an enormous amount of data and being transcribed as we speak. However, this 'knowledge transfer' makes me a little sceptical, it's almost benevolent. Why not wait until all our Right to Lives are dead then take us out en masse and end the matter? If they leave us, even with sub-light technology, we will always pose a potential threat to their stated long-term goals."

"*Perhaps. Or it could be they are doing to us what we've done to the bioadapts. If the speed of light is to be our limit, how far will we be able to progress or evolve? In fact, one could argue that keeping thirty-seven worlds cohesive or even loosely cooperative will prove a challenge in a sub-light scenario; inevitably leading to fragmentation and probably regression.*"

On one hand Magambál knew that the Admiral was simply pushing back testing her conviction. On the other, the 'solution' to the hybridisation problem was above top secret so her mentioning it in her presence meant they both knew she knew.

"When they arrive, the discussion will be transmitted directly to parliament on Earth and all system governments," Nagy informed her.

He was also telling her that what was being said now was off the record, so to speak, therefore be frank. "Everything about this is off key; if we're so insignificant to them why invest any time or energy in us?"

"You believe they have an ulterior motive? What?"

"Ulterior motives, Ma'am. I think we can hurt them and keep hurting them. That hurt will only increase as we learn more and adapt. Despite the obvious technological gap, we've learned that their power sources are magnetars. Now we know it's possible, how long do you think it will take us to be able to do the same? Centuries? Decades? They want to con us into plateauing our technology like we plateau the populations on most planets."

The Platinum Stinger and the Guardsman entered accompanied by both Naomi and Edzai. Magambál supressed a smile, she guessed if she'd been in their shoes, she wouldn't want to miss this either. She waved them all into seats.

"Ladies and gentlemen," the Field Martial addressed the infantry. *"I have one simple question for you: why should we believe you?"*

The four looked around at each other before the Guardsman Bashe eventually spoke. "MMBs don't really get the concept of lying but they do understand uncertainty. They don't get why we might not understand and accept that for them intelligent life, even in the shadow realm, has value. They invested time, effort and, more importantly, energy in trying to establish communication with us. They also offered to transfer us to the Realm of True Existence because of our intelligence. Our subsequent actions, especially our refusal to reduce our numbers to be proportional to available resources, demonstrate that we are not sufficiently evolved. But they do understand uncer..."

"They understand that we toasted one of their neutron stars. We did it once so we can do it again. And it's nonsense to say we won't be able to seek and destroy them!" Magambál felt there had been more than enough of this defeatist drivel.

Bashe stared back, assessing her as if to check whether he would be barked at, or not. "Well, we'll only be able to detect a magnetar when it's partially submerged in our realm... The MMBs only do that when they're transferring something to or from our realm that they wanted to keep functioning and alive."

The Platinum Stinger nodded then diplomatically leant forward to support his colleague. "We think that to establish us in their realm, all our atoms were somehow transformed to missing matter atoms and then, obviously, converted back. That probably took a lot of energy which could explain the submersion of..."

The female Guardsman, Thariyan, suddenly sat forwards. "Without Earth you would cease to be. Ebury is your next most Earth-like planet: you call it the Garden Planet. You deliberately limit your industry, agriculture, and impact on the local ecosystem there. Yet you have chosen not to restrict your numbers across all ecosystems and habitats. There are no Right to Life on Ebury's primary moon, Ontiel. If Ontiel were to be gone, Ebury's axil tilt would wobble severely, leading to the extinction of complex life. Ontiel will remain but on Ontiel you will not."

It took a few seconds comms-lag before the Admiral demanded, *"Guardsman Thariyan, what the hell are you on about?!"*

Thariyan looked genuinely startled. "I just remembered that and felt compelled to blurt it out, Ma'am."

"Ma'am", the Platinum Stinger began with untypical timidity, "I think to do what they just did, talk to us directly, put them in a serious energy deficit, I wouldn't just blow it off."

"I agree," Bashe said as he looked at his wives for confirmation and support. "This is something new that they've cobbled together from being exposed to us in their realm."

"*OK, but what has Ebury or Ontiel got to do with the price of bread?*" The Admiral checked herself, clearly realising that only someone from Earth would 'get' the vernacular. "*What has Ebury got to do with us transitioning to sub-light?*"

Again, all four soldiers exchanged looks but none seemed to have the answer. Magambál was about to suggest that Thariyan statement was gibberish and that she should have another stab at explaining whatever it was that was going on between her ears... Nagy held up his hand as if for silence while obviously intently reading a screen at his end. Nearly a minute and a half passed in silence then Akobundu-Tan also became preoccupied in viewing something at her end. It was close to fifteen minutes of nervous anticipation before either of them spoke.

"*Parliament is going to throw in the towel.*" Field Martial Nagy was clearly speaking only to the Admiral.

"*That was outright unprovoked aggression, and a first direct strike. We can't give in to that!*"

Thariyan suddenly jumped to her feet. "You had doubt, now you have been given belief. If you evolve far beyond your current condition, we will reconnect." Then the Guardsman looked around as if surprised to find herself standing and abruptly sat.

Several seconds passed before Akobundu-Tan asked the Field Martial. "*Intimidation?*"

Field Martial Nagy shrugged in response. "*All the civilian stations have just abruptly disconnected from this feed. I suspect they believe they've heard enough; that we have nothing further to add and it's time for them to act with a modicum of urgency.*" Then he addressed the group, "*SitRep from Ebury: in the last ten minutes or so, everything manufactured and 'everyone' on Ontiel has been observed to have disintegrated, or more accurately de-coalesced, just as Omega Zero Three had. The government have decided to set in motion plans and a path to a sub-light society.*"

"One strike against a population centre and we're suddenly terrorised into capitulation?!" Magambál was surprised at just how enraged she felt.

"Parliament is wetting themselves," Field Martial Nagy sounded only a smidgen less incensed.

"Short of a coup how do we stop them?" Akobundu-Tan pondered aloud then sitting erect slammed her hand, palm down, on her conference table. *"I'm just repeating myself, but we can't just give in to this!"*

The Platinum Stinger deliberately turned to the Admiral. "Ma'am, having been exposed to us in their realm, the MMBs have obviously burned up energy in dialling-in to human-level fidelity of perception. This is significant because our perception is substantially different to theirs. What I mean is, I don't think you should interpret what happened on Ontiel as a threat or intimidation: that's what it would mean if a human did it."

"You will hear of us no more," the Guardsman Heye, seemingly surprised at her own words, announced to no one in particular.

Before the Admiral could respond to Heye or the Stinger, Bashe addressed the Field Martial. "Sir, you asked, 'Why should you believe us?'. The MMBs have shown, at our level of perception, that they can eliminate the entire population of a planet without disturbing a blade of grass. And they have done so *only* because we showed signs of doubt."

The End

INTERDICTOR

ISBN 978 0 9506087 8 1

For decades, Earth's Attack Cruisers have taken a pounding from an undefeatable enemy. An enemy so alien and so incomprehensible Earth's armies are close to utter devastation; clueless as to how to challenge the impending annihilation of the human race.

For the first time in the twenty-seven-year war the enemy has placed a base of operation on a planet and Admiral Ezocaagbo Akobundu-Tan is willing to risk the destruction of her fleet in order to get one man on to that planet, Lume, a highly trained special forces operative. He is also a Stinger, a human adapted for a single purpose - to kill...

ARMOUR

ISBN 978 0 9526287 9 8

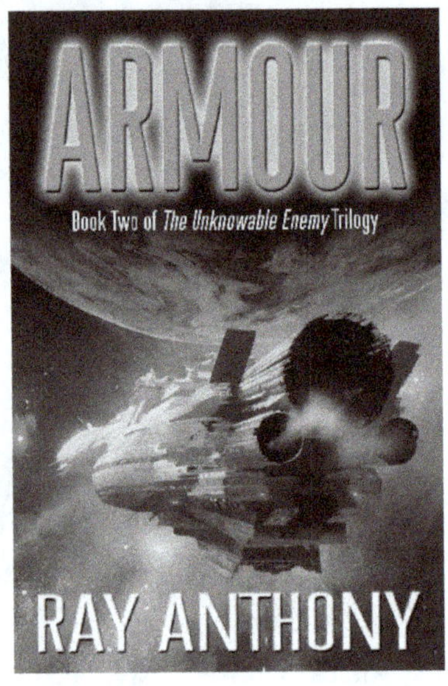

In a war to end all wars the ultimate armour is not what you think...

The war against their unknowable enemy – 'The Bulges' - rages on, for many of the soldiers battle is the only life they have known or will ever know. As a new wave of attacks devastates their fleets and destroy planets in humanity's battle for survival the best of the very best soldiers are enlisted into a secret carder.

The Guardsman is an exceptional soldier not just for his skill but something more…

PILOT

ISBN 978 0 9506087 6 7

The Explorer Corps' spaceship *Arabia* has the distinction of being the ship that has travelled the farthest distance from Earth. Eight days ago, Earth lost communication with the *Arabia*. The spacefighter, *Baddest*, is one of a pair of spaceships that, at more than fifty miles long are the largest machines ever built. *Baddest* is normally crewed by the Air Force's Ace Crew II but for this mission the crew is supplemented by the Navy's Special Combat Team Alpha. The Navy and Air Force are bitter space-borne rivals.

Mission: To find the vessel *Arabia* or to establish, beyond reasonable doubt, her fate and that of her crew.

EMPRESS

ISBN 978 0 9506087 4 3

She was the only one who could reunite the Empire and restore to its citizens the security that this brought. Without any doubt she was, singularly, the most important being alive. She and her cousin were the last of an Imperial bloodline.

But her cousin could not easily supplant her. For Hial to sit on the Imperial throne she would need to be victorious in a bitter and bloody war. Such a war was to be avoided if at all possible. Therefore, the primary task for Empress Morturina I, and those who served her, was to ensure her survival - at least until she had borne an heir to the Imperial throne.

But war was inevitable...

All Woman

ISBN 978 0 9506087 2 9

There you are getting on with your life. When up pops THE blast from the past... The dim distant past - not seen, not heard of in eight years - but there he is. He's telling you the story: 'Sorry I dumped you but having trashed all my subsequent relationships, I've finally come to realise that you are the one for me, we should be together.' It just so happens that he was the love of your life and it also happens that things are more than complicated...

What would you do?

INTERFACE

ISBN 978 0 9506087 7 4

It's the 80's. Clare is white, Patrick is black. They are from entirely different worlds, *but* when they met, they fell madly in love - perhaps opposites do attract. Now they plan to get married.

A straightforward proposition, right?

Well, maybe not. Set against them and their wishes are a host of 'interested parties': Clare's sister, Emma. Patrick's best friends, Harry and Nathan, and his ex-girlfriend, Otis. And of course, their parents want to have a say as well.

All the ingredients for a delightfully outrageous exploration of the *Interface* between: black men and white women; black men and black women; the maturity (or immaturity of men); strong personalities domination of weaker personalities.

Will love conquer all?

*There are many books written for women about the pregn[ancy &]
childbirth phenomenon. There doesn't seem to be much in this p[...]
literature for men. It's about time there was!"* - Ray A.

Thinking Man's Guide to Pregnancy, Childbirth & Fatherhood [(ISBN
978 0 9526287 3 6) provides a male's tongue-in-cheek perspective [...]
phenomenon - a humorous slant on all things an expectant father ne[eds to]
know but is too afraid to ask.

Disclaimer
Ray Anthony makes no claims to having any special qualifications for writing such a book,
apart from having been there, seen it, and done it!